PRAISE FOR THE BOOKS OF
#1 INTERNATIONAL BESTSELLING AUTHOR
KERK MURRAY

Since the Day We Kissed

"Murray nails the bittersweet nostalgia of first love. I'm pretty sure I just felt every emotion known to mankind."

— Reader Review

"The plot twists in this book caught me off guard in the best way possible. They kept me on my toes without sacrificing the emotional core of the story."

— Reader Review

"This is the first romance I've read written by a male and won't be my last by this author. His take on romance was surprisingly insight-ful—you can't help but cheer for Kara and

Ethan.”

— Reader Review

“The best story in the series by far!”

— Reader Review

“I can’t wait to read more Kerk Murray books! He’s my favorite new-to-me author.”

— Reader Review

“I absolutely adore Hadley Cove! It felt like I was returning to my hometown.”

— Reader Review

Since the Day We Fell

“Hadley Cove feels like a character in itself. It’s a place that feels both real and magical and one that I never want to leave.”

— Reader Review

"Kerk has a gift for capturing the nuances of human emotion. I found myself stopping to highlight several passages."

— Reader Review

"I've been a fan of Kerk's work since *Pawprints On Our Hearts*, and *Since the Day We Fell* did not disappoint."

— Reader Review

Since the Day We Danced

"Murray's writing is simply gorgeous."

— The Book Commentary

"An emotional rollercoaster that will make you fall in love with love all over again."

— Reader Review

"A beautiful escapist Nicholas Sparks type romance."

— Reader Review

Pawprints On Our Hearts

"Animal lovers will feel connected to Murray's almost spiritual awakening and admire his devotion to following his heart, even in the face of tremendous sacrifice. This touching memoir overflows with intense emotion."

— Booklife by Publishers Weekly

"A deeply moving memoir... one of the best books that capture the connection between human beings and dogs... *Pawprints on Our Hearts* inspires a love for animals while exploring the painful edges of the human heart in need of love and healing."

— The Book Commentary

"A powerful and emotional story."

— Alyson Sheldrake, Bestselling author of "Kat the Dog"

BY KERK MURRAY

Pawprints On Our Hearts
Since the Day We Danced
Since the Day We Fell
Since the Day We Kissed
Since the Day We Wished
Since the Day We Left
Since the Day We Promised

Since the Day We Kissed

KERK MURRAY

Since the Day We Kissed

Hadley Cove Sweet Romance: Book 3

Magnolia Press
Savannah

Magnolia Press
785 H King George Blvd
Ste D Box 13 -1016
Savannah, GA 31419

Library of Congress Cataloging-in-Publication Data

Names: Murray, Kerk, author.
Title: Since the Day We Kissed/ Kerk Murray.
Description: First edition. | Savannah: Magnolia Press, 2024.
Identifiers: LCCN 2024920572 | ISBN 9798985116182 (paperback) | ISBN 9798985116175 (hardcover)

Printed in the United States of America

To those who believe their best days are behind them. May you find the courage to create new beginnings from old endings—this one's for you.

Before You Begin...

You're invited to join my private Facebook Reader Group, where you'll make new book friends, meet other animal lovers, and be the first to know about new releases, book clubs, and special deals.

Join today:
Kerk Murray's private Facebook Reader Group

facebook.com/groups/779562103953550

Story Playlist

Listen on your favorite music streaming platform.

kerkmurray.com/products/sincethedaywekissedplaylist

Kara's Listens

1. "But Daddy I Love Him" — Taylor Swift

2. "Born to Fly" — Sara Evans

3. "Everywhere" — Michelle Branch

4. "Complicated" — Avril Lavigne

5. "Unwell" — Matchbox Twenty

6. "Kiss Me" — Sixpence None the Richer

7. "Don't Speak" — No Doubt

8. "Girl on Fire" — Alicia Keys

9. "Homegrown" — Zac Brown Band

10. "Are You Gonna Kiss Me Or Not" — Thompson Square

Ethan's Listens

1. "Red Dirt Road" — Brooks & Dunn

2. "American Soldier" — Toby Keith

3. "Iris" — Goo Goo Dolls

4. "Here Without You" — 3 Doors Down

5. "Summer of '69" — Bryan Adams

6. "Wherever You Will Go" — The Calling

7. "Photograph" — Nickelback

8. "How to Save a Life" — The Fray

9. "Then" — Brad Paisley

10. "Making Memories of Us" — Keith Urban

Dear Reader,

I'm thrilled to welcome you back to Hadley Cove for the third book in this series.

As I wrote this story, I found myself reflecting on the nature of love itself—how it can withstand time and distance, how it can heal wounds we thought would never mend.

You'll meet Kara and Ethan, whose journeys unfold through missed opportunities and unspoken truths, revealing the quiet strength it takes to confront the past and the courage required to open our hearts once more.

My hope is that as you wander through Hadley Cove alongside Kara and Ethan, you'll feel the sand between your toes, taste the salt on the air, and perhaps recognize a piece of your own heart in their experiences. I invite you to consider your own paths not taken, the words left unsaid, and the power we all have to rewrite our stories. May their journey inspire you to believe in the possibility of new beginnings, no matter where life has taken you.

Thank you for being a part of this incredible adventure and for joining me in creating a more compassionate world for all living beings, one heartwarming story at a time.

Your support through reading and sharing this series, along with your kind words in messages and reviews, means more than I can express. I'm forever grateful.

Don't forget to check out the extras I've included at the front and end of the book, created with you in mind.

♡ Kerk

"In a universe of ambiguity,
this kind of certainty comes only once,
and never again, no matter how many
lifetimes you live."

—Robert James Waller, *The Bridges of Madison County*

Prologue

Twenty-Two Years Earlier

Hadley Cove, Georgia

How did this happen?

The salty tang of the ocean filled the air alongside the distant cries of seagulls overhead. Kara's heart pounded. Her dad was going to kill her—and Ethan, too. Clutching the thick woolen blanket to her body, Kara leaned over and placed her hand on Ethan's shoulder.

"Ethan, wake up!"

His eyes fluttered open, then closed again. "Hmph?"

She shook his shoulder. "We gotta go. My dad's gonna freak when he finds out I didn't come home."

"Huh? What?" Ethan's eyes opened again.

"We stayed out all night. We fell asleep."

Ethan propped himself up on his elbows and blinked a

few times, taking in the secluded beach cove. His eyes crinkled, lips curving into a slow, contented smile as he gazed at Kara. "Well, good morning, gorgeous. I suppose we got a little carried away last night, huh?"

"Very!" Kara nodded rapidly, her eyes wide and her breath coming in short, sharp bursts. She pulled out her phone, but the screen was blank. Dead. "Ethan, what time is it? Can you check your phone?"

Ethan patted his pockets, his brow furrowing. "Uh, about that ... It fell in the water last night. We couldn't find it. Remember?"

Kara's eyebrows leaped toward her hairline, her jaw dropping as if unhinged. Her stomach plummeted as the gravity of their situation sank in. "Shoot! We need to grab our things and—"

"Looks like I'm phone shopping today." Ethan grabbed Kara's hand, pressing a kiss to the back of it. "Don't stress, babe. It's still early. We've got time."

Before Kara could say anything, Ethan sat up, cupped her face and met her lips with his as if nothing else mattered. She kissed him back as if she believed it, too.

As they parted, lips tingling from the shadow of their kiss, Kara rested her forehead against his. "Ethan, seriously. We really need to get going."

"All right, all right." He scrubbed his face with his hands. "I'm up." He reached over and grabbed his T-shirt from the sand. Dusting it off, he pulled it over his head and let out a yawn.

Kara snatched up her bag, sending a spray of fine sand into the air. She shoved the beach towels inside—the damp, gritty fabric rough against her fingers in her frantic rush. "We should've packed some of this stuff last night," she said, mostly to herself. "Have you seen my shoes?"

"I don't know ... maybe up near the grass? I think that's where I left mine." Smoothing back his blonde locks, Ethan got to his feet and stretched. "Can't believe the sand fleas didn't eat us alive out here."

"They should've," Kara said, shaking her head and scowling. "Would've been payback for being so irresponsible."

"Let's not call it irresponsible. I prefer—daring. Or adventurous." He snaked a hand around her waist, pulling her in for another kiss.

"My dad. Our boss. He won't see it that way." Kara smiled as she pressed her hands against Ethan's firm chest, pushing him away. "And stop distracting me. We've gotta focus."

"Come on, distracting you is what I do best." He reached for her again, but she stepped away, just missing the path of his outstretched arm, and began gathering more of their things.

"Ugh, these sandwiches have been sitting out all night." She grabbed a soggy PB&J half-wrapped in a piece of wax paper, then stuffed it into her bag. "Gross!"

Ethan waved his hand dismissively. "No biggie. Who cares about the sandwiches? I'm here for you."

"Uh-huh." Kara shook her head. "Now come on, help me pack up."

"Sun's barely up." Ethan grabbed one of the blankets and shook the sand off it. "You think your folks are even awake?"

Kara considered his question for a moment before responding. "Maybe." She grabbed the blanket from his hands and folded it. "But I'd rather not wait to find out. Can you hurry? And don't forget your camera."

Kara pointed at the Polaroid camera that Ethan had brought with him, lying on top of the sand.

"I know, I know." He leaned in and pressed a quick kiss to her nose. "But hey, before we go, let's take a picture. That's why I brought the camera, after all."

"Ethan." Kara's voice took on a pleading note.

"It'll just take a sec, I promise." He paused, grinning. "Two seconds, tops. We forgot to take them last night."

Kara tilted her head back, her eyes narrowing against the pale light of the rising sun. Her gaze followed a pair of pelicans skimming low over the water, their wings grazing the surface. A memento from what was probably the best night of her life would be worth the delay.

Her attention drifted back to Ethan. "Fine. But hurry."

"Alright, let's get one like this." Draping his arm across Kara's shoulders, he pulled her in close and held the camera out in front of them.

Click.

The camera flashed.

Kara blinked.

"Wait! I think my eyes were closed." She looked up at Ethan. "Can we take another?"

Ethan grinned. "Of course." He carefully tucked the first photo into his shirt pocket.

"Here, get one like this." Kara pulled his arm around her, resting her head on his chest.

Click.

Ethan slipped the second photo into his pocket alongside the first. "Ooh, and then one maybe like this?" He leaned down and kissed Kara on the cheek.

Click.

After securing the third photo, Ethan readied the camera again.

"How about we look into each other's eyes?" Kara asked, tipping her chin up to his face.

Click.

Ethan quickly pocketed the fourth photo before dipping his head. "How about a candid?"

"A candid? How's that supposed to work?"

"Like this!"

Ethan reached down and tickled the small of her back.

"Ah!" Kara let out a squeak. "You know that's where I'm the most ticklish!"

He started laughing. "I know."

Kara giggled as he tickled her again.

Click.

Kara held up her hand. "Okay, that's enough. How many did you get?"

Ethan carefully set the camera down, then pulled out the Polaroids from his pocket, each in various stages of development. He counted them quickly. "Five. Now we have to wait and see how they turned out."

"Ethan!"

"Chill. It'll just take a sec."

Kara crossed her arms, one eyebrow arching high. She stared at Ethan, unblinking, her foot creating a soft thump as it tapped against the sand. "A second. Two at the most?"

He waved the Polaroids back and forth. "We have to make sure they came out all right. Don't wanna get home and find out they're all duds."

"Fine, you can wait. But I'm gonna keep packing."

"Almost there." Ethan held them out. "And—there we go. See? That didn't take long."

Kara dropped her bag and stepped toward Ethan. "Let's have a look."

Ethan drew her into a side hug, holding the Polaroids out between them.

"Ugh, look at that one. My eyes are closed." Kara pulled it from the stack. "But you look cute in it. So, I'm keeping it."

Ethan smirked. "Okay, well then, I'm claiming this one. You look absolutely stunning here."

Kara's eyes lingered on the second photo, drinking in every detail. There she was, nestled against Ethan's chest, her long chestnut hair all messed up from the sea breeze. It should've looked awful, but somehow … it didn't? The image showed her in a way she rarely saw herself—carefree, radiant, and undeniably happy. Her usual self-consciousness had vanished, replaced by a girl who seemed to glow from within. It was a snapshot of pure, uncomplicated love—the kind she'd always dreamed of but never quite believed she'd find. "You really think so?"

"Definitely. In my completely honest opinion, you look gorgeous in every single one. Even the blinky ones."

Kara rolled her eyes. "If you say so. Looks like the rest are pretty blurry, though."

"Yeah, there's always a few duds. It happens."

"Well, I guess you were right. At least we both got a good one out of it." She picked up her bag and slipped the Polaroid into the side pocket. "But now we seriously need to go."

"All right, let's get you back." Ethan took the bag from Kara's hands and slipped it onto his shoulder. "Did we forget anything?"

Kara glanced around, her eyes scanning the grassy area where they had been. A few stray items caught her attention: a water bottle, a couple of napkins, and some litter that didn't belong to them. She hurriedly picked them up, adding them to the bag. "I think we've got everything now."

Ethan grinned. "Glad one of us has an eye for detail."

"Always good to leave a place better than we found it," Kara said, smiling as she adjusted her bag. "All right, let's go."

As they walked back to Ethan's blue Chevy truck and hopped inside, Kara's teeth chewed at her bottom lip. Excuses for her overnight absence spiraled through her mind, each more far-fetched than the last, crumbling under the weight of her dad's inevitable scrutiny. Her heart raced as she pictured the vein throbbing in his temple, his voice booming as he demanded an explanation. And if he ever found out she had been with Ethan—she shuddered to think of the consequences.

"Try not to worry," Ethan said as he pulled onto the road. "Everything will be fine."

Kara sighed. "I hope you're right … You know how my dad can be."

"He's probably still asleep. Don't worry, we'll be at your

house soon."

Kara leaned her head out of the window, the wind whipping through her hair. As they drove down the oak-lined street, she noticed the Spanish moss draping from the branches like wispy, gray-green curtains. The delicate tendrils swayed in the breeze, casting intricate shadows that danced across the windshield and the cobblestone sidewalks below. The sight was hauntingly beautiful, one that always took Kara's breath away, even in her anxious state. She watched the quaint shops and businesses pass by in a blur, her stomach twisting with each familiar landmark.

They were less than a minute from her house, and her pulse quickened as Ethan's truck rumbled down the familiar street.

"Hey, don't park out front," she told him. "Drop me off a few houses down—just to be safe."

"Sure thing." Ethan slowed and pulled the truck to a rolling stop two houses down from hers. Taking the keys out of the ignition, he turned to her. "Wanna hang out later today?"

Kara's eyes darted down the road to her parents' bedroom windows. Fingers fidgeted with the hem of her shirt, twisting the fabric as she scanned for any signs of movement. The curtains were drawn tight. The darkened glass revealed nothing, yet the sight sent her heart galloping in her chest. Her palms turned slick and cold with sweat. "I mean, I'd love to, but—" She took a breath and forced an exhale, "it kinda depends on how things go when I get inside."

Ethan took her hand, pulling her across the seat toward

him. "I can come with you, talk to your dad. Smooth things over."

A short, nervous chuckle bubbled up from Kara's throat before catching on to her vocal cords. "Are you kidding? He'd straight up strangle you if you walked into my house right now. Bad idea. No, best I deal with this myself." She looked over at him. "Call me later, yeah? When you get your new phone?"

"Of course," he said, with a roguish half-smile that made her heart skip a beat.

Leaning forward, Ethan closed the distance.

Kara's eyes fell shut, the darkness behind her lids filling with bursts of color. Then the world around her faded away until all that existed was the gentle pressure of Ethan's lips on hers, the heat of his breath mingling with her own, the hard planes of his chest pressed against her soft curves. They were two halves of a whole.

She tried to push down the nagging feeling that this moment of bliss was the calm before the storm. But even as she lost herself in Ethan's embrace, the niggling sense of unease remained, like a splinter lodged beneath her skin.

Then, as if a bucket of ice-cold water had been dumped over her head, her muscles tensed, her body went rigid, and her eyes snapped open. The dreamy haze of passion evaporated in an instant.

Her dad.

She needed to go inside.

Now.

As she broke the kiss, Ethan cupped Kara's chin, tilting her face up to meet his gaze. His touch was featherlight, yet it seemed to burn against her flushed skin, igniting a flurry of butterflies in her stomach. The intensity of his piercing blue eyes left her breathless.

"I love you. You know that, right? I'll love you forever, Kara," he whispered.

He spoke with a fierce conviction that she felt reverberating in every bone of her body. It filled her up, consuming her wholly and completely in a way she had never experienced before.

All she could do was nod while overcome and unable to find her voice.

"I know," she finally whispered back, her voice catching with the swell of feelings. "I love you too, but I really have to go."

Reluctantly, she slid back over to her side of the truck and reached for the door handle, already missing his touch and closeness. "You better call me."

Before she could jump out, he stretched across and grasped her small hand in his, entwining their fingers together. "You know I will."

1

Kara

Present Day

Friday

EVERYTHING HAD FINALLY CAUGHT up to her.

Kara Walker's fingers trembled over the keyboard.

She refreshed the page three times, hoping for a different result.

But the numbers didn't lie.

They only confirmed her worst fears.

Second Chance Animal Rescue was at full capacity.

She stared at the screen, heart sinking as she scrolled down the lengthy list of recent intakes. Outside her window, May flowers bloomed, oblivious to the crisis unfolding within these walls. For nearly two decades, she'd *nev-*

er turned away a single stray, but now they were arriving faster than she could find them new homes.

The harsh reality settled in her gut: The next abandoned soul to land on her doorstep would be the first she'd have to turn away.

Unable to bear the sight any longer, Kara minimized the spreadsheet with a shaky breath. The old office chair groaned as she pushed it back, its mismatched wheels snagging on the uneven floor. She rose, stretching her back as her stiff joints popped. Then with practiced ease, she navigated the obstacle course of her office-turned-storeroom. Towers of dog food bags and cleaning supplies loomed over her as she wove between them, their presence a constant reminder of the countless lives depending on her care.

As Kara reached for the door, a stack of folders began to topple. Kara's reflexes kicked in, and she lunged, catching them midair. With a sigh, she placed them back on the shelf, then wondered for the hundredth time if she'd ever get proper storage.

The lobby air enveloped her the moment she stepped inside—astringent disinfectant warring with the earthy musk of kibble. It was the rescue's signature scent, one that often clung to her clothes long after her workday had ended. Kara's shoes scuffed against linoleum that had seen better days, each step releasing a faint whiff of pine-scented floor cleaner.

As she arrived at the door to the kennel area, Kara paused, gathering her thoughts before plunging into the heart of the rescue. With a determined push, she opened the door.

A chorus of barks, whines, and a lone shrill yap welcomed her as she entered the cavernous room lined with rows of fenced-in enclosures, each housing dogs of every imaginable size and breed. She walked down the first row of kennels, peering in each one.

How had it come to this?

Kara stopped at the fourth kennel and kneeled.

A scruffy cocker spaniel mix with soulful brown eyes lay curled on a flannel blanket, her four wriggling puppies nestled against her belly, nursing at her side. Kara smiled, recalling the afternoon the pregnant dog had been brought in and the relief she had felt that the little lady had given birth safely at the rescue—but this also meant that there were now four new puppies needing adoption.

Sighing, Kara stood and continued down the row.

Kara wondered if the rescue would make it to the next month—or, for that matter, if she would. The shortage of volunteers only exacerbated the problem. With fewer hands to help, Kara worked around the clock, her own health and well-being taking a backseat to the needs of the animals. The physical toll was evident in her aching muscles and the dark circles under her eyes, but it was the emotional strain that weighed heaviest.

Caught in an endless cycle of day-to-day crises, her fundraising efforts and strategic plans to move the rescue forward felt like distant dreams she could barely bring herself to think about, let alone implement. Being at full capacity meant more than just a lack of space for additional animals. It meant skyrocketing costs across the board. The food bill alone had doubled in the past month. Veterinary costs were spiraling out of control—routine check-ups, vaccinations, and unexpected emergencies had depleted their meager savings at an alarming rate. Even basic supplies like cleaning products and bedding were becoming luxuries they could scarcely afford.

The once-bustling adoption events had dwindled to sparsely attended gatherings. Potential fosters and adopters seemed few and far between. Even those who showed initial interest often hesitated when Kara outlined the true costs and resources required for proper animal care, their excitement dimming into uncomfortable silences and polite retreats as the reality of long-term commitment sank in.

What was she going to do?

Kara had exhausted every avenue, including reaching out to other rescues to see if they could take some of her animals—even temporarily—but that lifeline had dried up as well. Her inbox was a graveyard of well-meaning rejections. Just this morning, she'd received an email from Loving Hands Rescue in the next town over, confirming that they were also at capacity. It was the same story with Paw Pals last week, and Hopeful Hearts the week before that. Even Whisker Wishes, two counties away, had turned her down last month. Full kennels, strained budgets, and overworked staff—it was the same story everywhere she turned. The pattern was clear: Every rescue in the area was facing the same uphill battle, leaving Kara with the unsettling truth that help wasn't coming.

Why were there so many animals in need of a home right now?

Maybe it was time to expand—but how?

Second Chance Rescue didn't have a steady influx of cash; they couldn't set up more housing.

Kara wracked her brain for potential solutions, no matter how unpleasant. Desperate times called for desperate measures. Her mind drifted to her father, and for a moment, she considered asking him for help again. *No way. Not now. Never again.*

She could already hear his disapproving tone.

"Kara, when are you going to realize that playing Noah's Ark isn't going to pay the bills?"

"If you'd taken over the pharmacy, you wouldn't be drowning now."

"I built our family business. You're running a petting zoo."

The thought of facing his criticism now, when she was at her lowest point, made her stomach churn. She would figure this out on her own.

Grabbing a broom off the wall hook, Kara began sweeping the concrete walkway between the kennels, wincing at the accumulated fur and debris.

A bark erupted from the far end, followed by a splash. Kara rushed over to find Finn, Labrador mix, had knocked over his water bowl, creating a puddle that began to seep into neighboring kennels. As she mopped, the unmistakable smell of diarrhea wafted from another section. Kara groaned, steeling herself for the mess awaiting her. Hurrying to grab cleaning supplies, she was stopped short by an ear-splitting whine. She turned to see Max, the anxious husky, frantically pawing at his kennel door. To her horror, the latch was bending and could break at any moment.

One more disaster, she thought, and she might just lose it completely.

An hour later, Kara found herself back where she started, broom in hand. She'd managed to clean up the messes, calm Max, and reinforce his kennel latch.

With the sweeping finally complete, Kara moved on to the next task, changing out the bedding in each of the kennels. As she worked, her mind wandered back to her predicament.

Something's gotta give.

As she approached the last kennel at the end of the row, her eyes fell on the faded name tag affixed to the gate. *Benny*—the name belonging to a grizzled miniature schnauzer whose graying muzzle and world-weary eyes marked him as one of Second Chance Animal Rescue's most tenured residents. He had been overlooked at adoption events time and time again; mostly because of his age, Kara assumed, and that he was much slower these days, with the stiffness in his back legs giving him a little limp when he walked.

Kara stepped inside the kennel and closed the gate behind her. "Hey there, Benny," she whispered.

Benny stood from his blanket, stretching out his front paws as he took a few steps toward Kara, his tail wagging as she reached down to stroke his wiry hair. Once a rich salt-and-pepper, twelve years had softened Benny's distinctive schnauzer coat to a silvery-gray, lending him an air of quiet dignity and hard-earned wisdom.

"How are you doing, boy? Get a good nap in?" Kara's fingers found that perfect spot behind Benny's ear, and she grinned as his back leg thumped against the floor. "You're such a sweetheart, Benny. Don't you worry, we'll find someone who appreciates a distinguished gentleman like you."

He let out a whimper and closed his eyes.

Kara patted Benny's head. "I know, sweet boy. It won't always be this way. For now, let's get you a fresh blanket, okay?"

She laid out the fresh blanket, smoothing it with her hands. "There we go. All nice and clean." Reaching into her pocket, she grinned. "Look what I've got." She offered Benny two Riley's Recipe treats, which he devoured, his eyes brightening with a spark of his younger self.

Kara gave Benny one last scratch behind the ear. "Okay, buddy, you get some rest now. We'll go for a walk later, and in the meantime, I'll keep working on finding you the perfect home. Sound good?"

Benny let out one quick bark, then turned and laid back down on his new blanket. Smiling, Kara stood and stepped out of the kennel.

After she finished gathering all the old bedding, she headed over to the small laundry room and threw the blankets into the washing machine. As she started the load, she noticed a puddle forming at the base of the machine.

"You've got to be kidding me," Kara muttered, shoving a towel against the leak. It was a Band-Aid solution at best. She'd need to call a repair service—another expense she couldn't afford.

Once the load had begun, she walked back through the kennels and into her tiny office. Sinking into the creaky chair, Kara logged into her desktop computer and pulled up the daunting list of administrative duties she needed to finish. Just as she was about to dive in, her phone buzzed.

She smiled as she saw the face pop up on the screen, then picked it up and answered. "How are you, sweetie?"

Charlotte's voice came through the line. "I'm good! How are you?"

"Where are you? You sound far away."

"I'm driving," Charlotte said. "Just left. Heading back to Hadley Cove now."

"And you're talking on the phone? You need to pay attention to the road!"

"Mom, chill. I'm fine—I'm on speaker phone. Hands-free."

"Don't 'Mom' me. It's my job." Kara smirked and leaned back in her seat. "So, did you hear back from the internships you applied to?"

"Actually, yeah. Got a call from the clinic near campus."

Kara straightened. "That's the one you wanted, right? What'd they say?"

Charlotte sighed. "Well, they liked my application, but their internship program is full next semester."

"Oh, honey, I'm sorry."

"No, no, it's okay, Mom. I got an offer from another clinic outside of town. It's a bit of a commute, but I'm excited. They handle a lot of farm animals, so I'll get to tag along on some of those appointments and see what it's really like. Wasn't my first choice, but it's a good start. Things will work out. They always do. But I'm more excited about being home with you for the summer."

"Can't wait to have you home, too. And you know what? That's a really great perspective. I'm proud of you for seeing the silver lining." Kara's fingers traced the edge of the photo frame on her desk, her eyes drawn to the image of a younger Charlotte's smiling face. "When did my little girl grow into such a thoughtful, mature young woman?"

"I am pretty awesome, ain't I?"

"Humble too." Kara let out a chuckle. "I just know you're gonna be an amazing vet when you finish school."

"I hope so," Charlotte said. "But hey, it's starting to pour. Need to go. I'll be home in an hour—an hour and a half, tops."

"You sure you don't want to just wait it out? Maybe you can pull over until it passes. No need to rush getting here, honey."

Charlotte laughed. "Mom, I've driven in worse. I'll be fine, I promise."

Kara sighed, her frown deepening. "Well, be careful. Drive slow and keep your headlights on. It's getting dark. Okay?"

"Stop worrying."

"I know my old self worries too much, but that's what us moms do."

"Forty is *not* old!"

Kara chuckled. "If you say so."

"I do say so. But gotta go for real. Love you."

"I love you too, sweetie. See you soon."

As the call disconnected, Kara set her phone down on the cluttered desk. The warmth of her daughter's voice lingered for a moment, and she smiled. For all the joy Charlotte had brought her, being a single mom had never been easy. There'd been countless nights lying awake wondering if she was giving Charlotte enough, if she was enough. The juggling act between work, bills, the rescue, and motherhood—it had felt impossible. But she'd done it. Somehow ...

Kara released a sigh, and her smile soon faded as her mind wrestled again with the mountain of challenges facing the rescue.

When Kara returned to the to-do list on her computer, her elbow accidentally nudged a stack of papers. As they slid, a familiar corner peeked out—the dog-eared edge of *Animal Rescue Stories*, the book her mother had read to her every night as a child. Kara gently pulled it free, running her fingers over the worn spine and yellowed pages. The book fell open to a well-loved chapter, and in an instant, she could hear her mother's soothing voice.

"Second chances aren't just for the animals we save; they're for all the hearts we heal along the way."

Smiling, Kara remembered how her mom would bring home stray dogs and cats—much to her father's disapproval, which only made her open her arms wider. She had a soft heart for all the poor, unwanted animals in the world, and that's how she lived her life until the day of the accident.

Kara's eyes fluttered shut, and in the darkness behind her lids, she saw that last day with startling clarity.

"Tomorrow, we'll start planning our own sanctuary. With all these strays, we need a proper home for them," her mom had said.

But tomorrow never came. Just a phone call, flashing lights, and heartache like nothing she'd ever known.

Tears stung her eyes, turning the world into a watery blur. She swallowed against the tightness in her throat. Her mom would've loved the rescue and all the work Kara had done in the community to give stray animals a safe haven. But now—what would her mom think of the problems she was facing? How would *she* fix it?

Losing the rescue would mean more than just giving up her life's work; it would be like losing her mother all over again. Coupled with this was the agonizing fear of letting down the animals who needed her—those abandoned souls who had nowhere else to go.

The weight of it all pressed down on Kara's shoulders, making it hard to breathe, but more of her mom's words echoed in her mind again.

"Remember, sweetheart, every setback is just a setup for a comeback."

Throwing in the towel wasn't an option.

Kara wiped away her tears with the back of her hand and squared her shoulders, ready to take on the task ahead. Over the years, in the space between heartache and hope, she'd discovered the truest measure of love—giving all, knowing the cost.

Turning back to her computer, Kara forced herself to focus. There was no time for her to get lost in her thoughts, not when she had a rescue at full capacity and volunteers to find. As she started typing out the list of supplies she would need for the upcoming adoption event, the soft chime of the front doorbell cut through the quiet of the office. A single bark rang out from the kennels, followed by another, and another, until the air was filled with excited woofs and howls.

Kara's heart raced.

This late? Who could be visiting the rescue now?

A new volunteer signing up? Part of her dared to hope, but the almost two decades of late-night emergencies had taught her to prepare for the worst.

Images flashed through her mind: a sodden cardboard box, whimpering puppies, a hastily scrawled note bearing a simple message: "Please help them. I can't."

This was more likely—always more likely—in this calling of endless heartbreak and healing that was both her blessing and her burden.

2

Ethan

ETHAN BENNETT WISHED HE were *anywhere* but here.

Thunder rumbled in the distance as rain battered the old house's metal roof, its sound echoing through the overgrown yard. Ethan's shoulders hunched as his thin shirt clung to his skin like a clammy second layer. Rivulets of water ran down his back as he hustled over to the passenger side of his blue Chevy and opened it.

"Hero. Come on, boy. Let's go."

The Australian Shepherd leaped from the truck with fluid grace, making a small splash in the puddle that had gathered around the vehicle. He barked, then sidled up to Ethan's leg. Reaching down, Ethan stroked Hero's drenched blue-merle-and-white coat, feeling warmth seep through the already soaked fur. The dog shook off the rain, droplets spraying into the air before disappearing into the waterlogged soil beneath them. Hero's peculiar gaze—one eye a sky blue, the other a warm brown—met Ethan's with an almost human-like questioning, as if silently chiding his master for forgetting a jacket.

Ethan smiled, then strained to see through the gray sheets of rain toward the house. As his eyes traced the contours of 237 Willow Creek Road, more than two decades seemed to dissolve like mist, leaving him feeling like that same uncertain teenager who had fled this town so long ago.

The peeling paint.

The crooked mailbox.

Vines choking the porch railing.

It looked exactly as he remembered—a ramshackle, dingy old mess—and now that his father was gone, it was his problem.

Great.

Ethan steeled himself and trudged toward the house. With each step, mud oozed around his boots, while Hero's paws left a trail of glistening prints. The porch groaned as they climbed the rotting steps, old wood bowing under their combined weight. Reaching the door, the key scraped against rust as Ethan jammed it into the lock, twisting and jiggling until it finally gave way with a click.

The door opened with a push.

"Here we go," Ethan muttered, giving Hero a quick pat.

The moment Ethan crossed the threshold, a wave of stale air hit him, carrying the unmistakable scent of mildew. Hero padded in behind him, sniffing cautiously, before settling onto a threadbare rug a few feet away. Ethan's nose wrinkled involuntarily as he scanned the living room, eyes drifting over the ancient television set, then to a bookshelf cluttered with old mystery novels and mismatched knick-knacks. The couch, worn and torn at the seams, sagged under its faded upholstery, revealing patches of yellowed foam beneath.

Absolutely *nothing* had changed.

Ethan moved through the living room into the kitchen, dropping his keys and phone on the counter as he used to when he lived here. He walked over to the fridge and opened it, unsure of what he'd find. It was mostly bare, with a few half-empty bottles of water on the middle shelf and an old jar of pickles in the door. He closed it and turned around, taking in the peeling wallpaper next to the stove.

A soft, persistent drip broke the silence. Ethan's eyes followed the sound to a small, dark stain spreading across the ceiling. A droplet swelled at the center of the patch before it released and splashed onto the floor. Another drop fell, then another.

Ethan grunted and grabbed an old pot from the cabinet below. The drip turned into a hollow *plink*. Each drop hitting the bottom of the pot filled the air, steady as a heartbeat.

Hero's ears perked, and he trotted over to investigate, nose twitching as he sniffed at the pot. Ethan absentmindedly scratched the dog's head.

The house felt heavier than it used to—like it had absorbed years of neglect along with the memories. He wiped his hands on his jeans and stepped into the hallway, heading toward a familiar wall.

Dust motes floated in the dim light as his gaze landed on a row of old photographs. The cheap plastic frames lined up like a visual timeline, each one a window into the boy he used to be. First grade, gap-toothed and hopeful. Fifth grade, gangly and bright-eyed. Seventh, awkward but determined. Tenth, a hint of the man emerging. And then the last—his senior portrait. That one wasn't even framed, just pinned up with a thumbtack.

His calloused fingers skimmed the edge of the crinkled, sepia-toned school portrait.

A cold nose nudged his hand, startling him from his reverie. Hero gazed up at him, tail wagging.

Ethan smiled, rubbing the dog's snout. "Yeah, boy. That was a lifetime ago."

He had been so sure of everything back then, his carefree grin radiating from the pictures. Before the military, before he had known the heartache that time could never mend.

Ethan let out a breath and approached the first door on the left—his old bedroom. He reached out and turned the knob ...

Everything was still there—his bed, his desk, his dresser, and even the baseball posters of the Chicago Cubs he'd hung on the walls. The room remained untouched, right down to the rumpled sheets on the bed.

Ethan paused before stepping onto the worn floorboards, crossing the room. He stopped in front of the dresser, where a thin layer of dust coated everything. With a hand, he wiped across the top, clearing away the layer that had settled over the years. Among the forgotten items, he found his old class ring and a Ryne Sandberg baseball card.

As he continued to examine the dresser's surface, his eyes traveled to a black frame, tilted face-down. He righted it, revealing a photo that hit him like a punch to the gut—him and his dad, both grinning in the stands at Wrigley Field.

Ethan's throat tightened. His father had never cared for baseball, but for one day, he'd pushed aside the bottle and taken Ethan to the game. It was a rare glimpse of the man his father could have been, a fleeting moment when everything had felt right.

Setting the frame back with a soft clink, Ethan's attention shifted to his old nightstand. There, beside a baseball-shaped lamp, sat his Polaroid camera. He lifted the camera, its familiar weight settling in his palms. As he turned it over, his mind drifted to the last time he used it.

All at once, it was as if she were right there beside him—Kara's smiling face pressed against his chest, her soft hair tickling his chin, carrying the faint scent of jasmine. The waves crashing on the beach. The warmth of their last kiss—and the promise he had made to call her.

He closed his eyes, remembering how the next day—everything had happened so fast—he enlisted in the army, and before he knew it, he was gone.

He didn't even tell her goodbye.

Across oceans and years, no matter how far he ran, that summer with Kara wasn't something he could just leave behind. It was part of him, something he carried everywhere.

Ethan swallowed hard, took a deep breath, and loosened his grip on the camera—and the memory—trying to push away the painful truth he never wanted to face: Sometimes the greatest acts of love are the ones that break our hearts, but we do them anyway.

After setting the camera back on the dresser, his attention shifted to the mirror hanging above, meeting the gaze of a forty-year-old man shaped by choices made and words left unsaid.

The stranger in the mirror blinked back at Ethan—familiar blue eyes now framed by crow's feet and tousled blonde hair streaked with silver. His gaze fell to the tattoos on his arm, each inked line a chapter of the life he'd lived since leaving this house—one dedicated to his fallen Rangers, which concealed a scar, and the other of Hero's paw prints.

Turning away from the mirror, Ethan left his bedroom and strode down the hall, peeking into the bathroom to survey the damage there. Surprisingly, it was relatively well-kept and free of clutter. His father may have been a fall-down drunk, but at least he wasn't a hoarder. A small win, Ethan supposed.

With a mix of dread and curiosity, he continued his tour to his father's bedroom.

The door was cracked.

He pushed it open and stepped inside with Hero.

At first glance, the room looked as Ethan remembered. When his vision adjusted to the dimness, he noticed new items on the walls. Nearing it, Ethan's breath hitched.

There, in a simple frame, hung his portrait—a younger version of himself, jaw set, eyes forward, and the crisp lines of his Army Service Uniform. Beside it, a newsprint screamed a headline he'd long tried to forget: *Hadley Cove Hero Awarded Silver Star.*

Pride, pain, and confusion warred within him as he stood, rooted to the spot.

Since leaving Hadley Cove twenty-two years ago, Ethan had changed his number and never called or returned—even after retiring from the military and settling in Virginia.

Not once.

After what his dad had done, who could blame him?

CRASH!

Ethan's head snapped up.

What was that?

He rushed to the window, cupping his hands around his eyes, hoping to see past the thick grime and dirt.

The only thing visible was the rain.

"Hero, with me," Ethan called out, hurrying down the hall until he reached the front door. He threw it open with one swift motion and rushed onto the porch.

Ethan descended from the porch, each footfall producing a wet, sucking sound from the saturated earth, Hero's soft paws pattering after him. Rain pelting them as Ethan shielded his eyes, squinting past his truck through the downpour.

At the edge of the road, his heart plummeted.

Stepping forward, he was transported to another time, another place ...

In an instant, the dreary rain vanished, giving way to a blinding, scorching light that seared Ethan's retinas. Coarse sand ground beneath his boots with each step. The humid air reeked of smoke, diesel fuel, and burned rubber.

Twisted hunks of metal littered the road before him, barely recognizable as a Humvee. Flames licked at the shredded tires, black smoke billowed into the sky. Ethan's mouth went dry as a strangled gasp clawed its way up his throat, erupting into a primal scream that shattered the surrounding air."Carter. Ramirez. Davis. No, no!"

His combat boots felt like lead weights as he forced himself to move closer. The heat rolled off the burning wreckage in suffocating waves. Sweat trickled down his back beneath heavy Kevlar. His rifle hung like an anvil in his hands.

BARK! BARK! BARK!

Ethan blinked, and the arid landscape receded, bringing the rain-soaked road back into focus. Hero released another bark, dispelling the lingering wisps of the memory.

Reality hit him with full force as red brake lights pierced through the storm, flashing like a beacon in the distance. He wasn't in Afghanistan; he was in Hadley Cove, and his body moved before his mind could catch up, legs pumping, Hero a gray blur at his side.

The air grew thick with the stench of gasoline and rain, an acrid cocktail that burned his lungs with each ragged breath.

This was far worse than he'd imagined.

Glass and metal shards were strewn across the road like shrapnel.

As he drew closer, his stomach dropped.

The twisted car came into view, crumpled against a large oak tree.

Hero bolted ahead, a streak of blue merle and white against the slick asphalt. The dog circled the wreckage, his frantic barks cutting through the storm's roar.

Heart pounding, Ethan surged forward, reaching for the driver's side door. He yanked it.

Stuck.

He tried again, this time with both hands.

The door wouldn't budge.

A string of curses hissed under his breath.

Ethan swiped the foggy window clear and pressed his forehead against the cool glass. The deflated airbag draped over the steering wheel like a discarded parachute, partially obscuring the driver's face, but not completely. Through the makeshift veil, he could see a young woman with her head lolling against the seat.

"Hey!" Ethan pounded on the window, hard enough to make his knuckles throb. "Can you hear me? Say something!"

No response.

Hero's barks turned into a whine before his ears pricked forward, head tilted as if he were trying to understand.

Ethan's heart slammed against his ribs as he shoved a hand into his pocket, fingers grasping for his phone.

Empty.

He checked his other pocket.

Still nothing.

Spinning around, he bit his lip and shot a desperate look in the direction of the house.

There it was, clear as day in his mind—his phone, lying useless on the kitchen counter—might as well be in another galaxy.

His gaze darted between the unconscious woman and the distant house.

He needed to call for help, but he couldn't just leave her here …

3

Kara

"MISSED YOU!" EMMA RUSHED toward Kara and pulled her into a hug.

Kara held her close for a moment. "It's so good to see you, Em!" She stepped back and crouched. "And you too, Riley boy." The golden retriever's fluffy tail swiped back and forth like a windshield wiper as he pushed his cool, wet nose into her palm. "Feels like only yesterday he was a stray here. Remember the day you took him home?"

Emma laughed, tugging gently on Riley's leash. "How could I forget? And now look at him—total diva."

"Well, he did win the Fall Festival Mascot Contest last year. He's basically a small-town A-lister."

"Don't remind him." Emma smiled, then gestured toward the parking lot. "Anyway, got some goodies for you. Come on."

Kara trailed the two to Emma's car. "Em, you didn't have to bring anything. Seeing you is enough."

"Oh, stop." She popped open the trunk, revealing two colorful boxes, then placed them into Kara's arms. "Here ya go."

Kara adjusted her grip as the weight tugged her arms down. "What are these? Bricks?"

"Only the latest and greatest flavor of Riley's Recipe treats. Banana and pumpkin. Sounds weird, I know, but trust me on this one."

"I'm honored," Kara said as they walked back into the rescue. She glanced at Riley with a knowing smirk. "Let me guess—he's already given these his seal of approval?"

"He's ob-*sessed*," Emma said. "Ain't that right, boy?"

Riley's haunches hit the ground with a thud, his tail sweeping an arc across the floor. His eyes ping ponged between Kara and Emma, ears perked forward, pink tongue peeking out.

"This dog." Emma chuckled, shaking her head. "Acts like I never feed him. He had two treats on the car ride over here."

"Another one won't hurt, right?" Kara winked at Emma.

Emma arched a brow. "All right. But if he gets fat, I'm blaming you." She slipped a treat from her pocket, holding it just out of reach, before his jaws snapped around it. With two quick chomps, the treat vanished. Riley licked his chops with a satisfied smack and eyes that were already searching for more.

Kara smiled warmly at the scene and set the boxes on the table. She opened one and pulled out one of the clear bags, tied with ribbon, then inspected it. "You baked them into hearts this time. Very cutesy."

"Aren't they?"

"The regulars are gonna love these."

Emma clapped her hands. "Well then, let's get these set up. Shall we?"

They began to unpack the boxes, arranging the treat bags on the display. Soon, the once-empty table was transformed into a colorful array of heart-shaped treats.

"There," Kara said, placing the final bag. "I think that's everything."

"Oh! I almost forgot!" Emma dashed to her car and returned with another large box, setting it on the table. "These are for the pups in the back. I made extra batches of the broken pieces and scraps. They may not be heart-shaped, but I'm sure the dogs won't mind."

"Em, it must have taken you hours to make all these. How much do I owe you?"

"Not a thing." Emma shook her head. "It's a donation to the rescue." Her voice softened. "Without you, I wouldn't have Riley. And without him—" She patted the display. "Well, none of this would exist. It's the least I can do."

Kara smiled. "I don't deserve you."

"You kidding me? I'm the lucky one here. You deserve all the wonderful things. I just happen to be one of them." Emma batted her eyes and tossed her auburn hair over her shoulder.

Kara pressed her lips together, trying to keep a straight face, but when their eyes met, they both giggled.

As their laughter subsided, Kara gave a quick nod toward the back. "Wanna see the pups?"

"Do you even have to ask? Lead the way."

As they walked through the double doors to the kennels,

the familiar sounds of the rescue surrounded them: dogs barking from their cages, the occasional clatter of a metal water bowl being nudged across the floor, and the low hum of the ventilation system working overtime to keep the place cool.

Emma looked up and down the aisles, her eyes scanning the rows of occupied kennels. "How many dogs are there?"

"With the new litter," Kara's gaze fell on the nearest kennel, "twenty-four."

Emma's eyes widened. "Whoa. I can't even imagine. Your volunteers must be working overtime to keep this place running, huh?"

Kara leaned back against the rough-textured wall. "Yeah, that'd be nice, wouldn't it?"

"What do you mean?"

Kara's eyes glistened, her lower lip trembling as she fought for control. For three ragged heartbeats, silence stretched between them. Then her composure crumbled, words spilling out in a rush. "Em, I-I don't even know where to start. Our volunteers have been dropping like flies—moving away, ghosting us, you name it. It's been like this for months now." Her voice cracked. "I'm trying to do everything myself, but I can't keep up. Adoptions are down, we're out of foster homes, and we hit capacity weeks ago. The bills keep piling up, our savings are nearly gone, and I—" She took a shaky breath. "I'm drowning here, Em. I love this place more than anything, but I don't know how much longer I can keep this up alone."

"Oh, Kara, why didn't you say something sooner? I had no idea things were this bad." Emma crossed the space between them in two quick strides, her arm settling around Kara's slumped shoulders.

Kara wiped her eyes with the back of her hand. "You've got your own stuff going on. Your business, your family." She sighed. "I didn't want to dump my problems on top of all that."

"Stop. Right now. You're family. Your problems are my problems." She glanced around the kennels. "What can I do to help tonight?"

Kara patted Emma's hand. "Thanks, I'm good for now. Bedding's changed, everyone's fed, and they've all had their outside time." She attempted a reassuring smile. "Just a rough patch. I'll figure it out."

Emma's eyes lit up. "Wait, the adoption event coming up—that's perfect! We can set up a recruitment booth. I'll take care of it—signage, talking to people, and whatever else we need to do to get you volunteers."

"Em, seriously, you don't have to—"

"It's done. I love you and we're gonna get you out of this mess."

Kara's eyes welled up again. "Love you too. You're the best."

"No, you are."

WOOF! WOOF! WOOF!

"Looks like we have a volunteer," Kara said with a grin. Emma laughed as they made their way toward the commotion at the last kennel on the first row, inscribed with the name *Benny.*

"Hey boy!" Kara unlocked the gate. "Wanna say hello?"

Riley's tail wagged as Benny stepped out of his kennel,

giving the retriever a sniff inspection.

"I think they like each other," Emma said, kneeling to pet Benny. "Wait a sec—isn't this the sweetheart that got adopted like three months ago?"

"Yeah, about that. They, uh, brought him back." Kara kneeled next to him.

Emma's jaw dropped. "You've got to be kidding me. Who would do that to this little guy?"

Kara's hand moved over Benny's coat gently, as if to comfort both the senior miniature schnauzer and her own frayed nerves. "I get life happens, but that wasn't the case here. They just changed their minds. As if he were a sweater that didn't fit right." Her eyes drifted to Benny's graying muzzle. "Don't get me wrong. I'm glad they brought him back and didn't dump him on the side of the road. It kills me though, Em. Benny's been through so much. He deserves a real home, a family that'll stick by him."

"Poor boy. Some people make me sick."

"I know. And that's why we do what we do." Kara cleared her throat, forcing a lighter tone, and switched her kneeling position to a sitting one. "But enough about my drama. Tell me about you. Anything new in your life?"

"Oh, you know, same old," Emma said, taking a seat on the ground. "Business is booming—turns out people really love overpriced dog treats." She chuckled. "Luke's been a godsend at the shop. Sometimes I think he enjoys it more than I do. And Jeremiah made the dean's list. Again!"

"That's amazing! All good news." Kara smiled.

"He'll be home for summer break soon. Bet I could convince him to lend a hand around here."

Kara laughed. "Don't you dare conscript that poor boy for rescue duty. He needs a break." She paused. "But, if he's offering—I wouldn't say no. Also, I'll have to tell Charlotte he's back. She'll be home tonight."

"Aww, tell her we said hey. And I'm sure he'd be more than glad to help. Oh, and you know Lisa and Noah's bed-and-breakfast? They got a new menu. We should totally check it out sometime. We're long overdue for a catch-up."

Kara shrugged. "Sounds great, if I can find the time."

"Oh, we're making it happen, missy. Even if I have to drag you out of here myself." Emma nudged Kara before Riley plopped all of himself onto her lap. "Ugh, you big lug. You are *not* a puppy anymore." She readjusted under his weight, then lowered her voice conspiratorially. "So, changing gears here. Whatever happened with that guy? You know, the one from the app?"

An awkward sound escaped Kara's throat, somewhere between a laugh and a groan. "Don't get me started on that train wreck."

Emma leaned in. "All aboard! Now, spill."

"Well, for starters, Mr. Six-Two is really Mr. Five-Nine. On a good day, in boots."

Emma winced. "A lot of men are self-conscious about their height. I mean, he seemed nice from what you told me, though."

"You mean a little too nice? You know what they say about things, or people, being too good to be true."

"Wait, what? How can someone be 'too nice'?"

Kara's voice dropped short of a whisper. "For starters,

he's married. And get this—his wife? She volunteered here. Once. Can you believe that?"

Emma threw her hands up. "Of course he is. Why are guys like this?"

"Right? Dating at forty feels impossible. It's like trying to find that one matching sock in the laundry basket. You know it's there somewhere, but all you keep finding are mismatched pairs and ones with holes in them."

"Who needs matching socks anyway? At least you know now what you don't want. But look, your Mr. Right is out there somewhere. He's probably just—lost. Or stuck in traffic. Or something ..."

"Yeah, probably in Alaska. Maybe I was meant to be alone forever." Kara let out a sigh. "It's fine, really. Between this place and everything else, who has time for dating anyway?"

Emma straightened. "All right, enough of that. You, my friend, are a total catch. I know you've got a lot on your plate, but that doesn't mean you don't deserve happiness. Your person *is* out there. And they'd be lucky to have you."

"I appreciate the pep talk, I really do. But right now?" She gestured around the kennel. "These guys need me. Finding them homes is my priority. Everything else can wait. It has to wait."

"Okay, okay. I get it." With a soft grunt, Emma pushed herself to her feet, her hand searching for Riley's leash. "So, I guess we'll get going so you can rest up. But if you need anything else—anything at all—you call me. Or text. Got it?"

Kara saluted. "Yes, ma'am."

Emma fixed Kara with a serious stare. "I mean it. Anytime, day or night. Promise me."

"I promise. Scout's honor and all that."

"Good. I'll see you at the adoption event." Emma reached out and hugged her. "Try not to work yourself to death before then, okay?"

Kara returned the hug. "I'll do my best. No promises, though." She grinned, then stepped back. "And thanks again for the treats."

"Don't mention it, girl. See ya."

"See y'all."

As the sound of Emma's footsteps faded into the lobby, Kara stretched, then walked to her office. She pushed open the door, immediately confronted by the organized chaos within. Stepping over a stack of donation forms, she sidled past towers of pet food bags then ducked under a dangling pet toy—narrowly avoiding a collision with a precariously balanced box of leashes. Then she shimmied between the filing cabinet and a mountain of towels before finally reaching her chair. Settling in, she took a determined inhale and faced the mountain of paperwork awaiting her.

She'd barely put pen to paper on a grant application when her phone's vibration cut through the quiet.

Another scam? Probably about extending my expired car warranty. If I had a dollar for every ...

She pressed the green button on the touch screen.

"Hey, who's this?"

A female voice asked, "Hello, is this Ms. Walker?"

"Yes, this is her."

"Ms. Walker, I'm the head ER nurse at Hadley Cove General. Is Charlotte Walker your daughter?"

"Yes, she is. What's going on?" The world seemed to tilt and blur around the edges for a moment as Kara's heartbeat thundered in her ears, drowning out all other sounds in the now too-quiet room. Her hand tightened around the phone and she steadied herself by gripping the edge of her desk with her free hand.

"There's been an accident."

A high-pitched ringing filled her ears. Her fingers, clumsy and uncooperative, struggled to maintain their grip on the phone. Charlotte's face flashed before her eyes—her daughter's smile, her laugh, the sound of her sweet voice she'd heard only a couple hours ago.

Kara's mouth opened, but no sound emerged.

"Ms. Walker?" The nurse's voice cut through the fog. "You should get up here as soon as you can."

4

Ethan

ETHAN SQUINTED AGAINST THE harsh glare of fluorescent lights as he and Hero entered the hospital lobby. A whoosh came from the doors sliding shut behind them, and a sprawling circular desk sat in the center ahead.

His throat tightened as he approached, each step heavier than the last.

"Excuse me," Ethan said, "there was a woman brought in earlier—car accident. I need to know if—"

The receptionist's eyes flicked from Ethan down to Hero. "Sir, is that a service animal?"

Ethan shifted his weight from one foot to the other, his hand moving to Hero's head. "Not officially, but he's my support—"

The receptionist's face softened. "I'm sorry, but only certified service animals are allowed in the hospital. You'll need to wait outside."

Ethan sighed. *What's this place have against support ani-*

mals?

Hero was just as good as any service dog. Heck, he'd saved Ethan's life in a war zone.

He leaned in. "Please, I just need to know if she's—"

"Sir, are you a family member?"

"No, but I was there when—"

The receptionist held up a hand, her voice sharpening. "I understand, but we have strict policies about patient privacy. Again, you'll need to wait outside."

What if the woman has no family?

The image of the woman waking up alone in an empty room flashed through Ethan's mind. Years in the military had taught him the value of rules. Most were good, or so he thought. But not this one.

"I understand." Ethan nodded, then turned on his heel and headed back toward the exit.

As he reached it, he glanced back, catching the receptionist's watchful gaze. With a resigned sigh, he went outside and hoped for a chance to gather more information. It was a small hospital, after all ...

Maybe her family will show up and I can speak to them out here.

At least the rain had stopped. Ethan spotted a bench near the entrance. He made his way over and sank onto it. From there, he could see every face that passed through the sliding doors.

It's gonna be a while.

Leaning back against the bench, Ethan scanned the near-empty parking lot. There was his truck, with a few others parked off to the side. He supposed that was a good thing. The quiet of the night was almost soothing.

A wail shattered the silence, and red lights strobed across the asphalt as an ambulance careened into the parking lot, its siren now a deafening howl. Ethan's pulse spiked as the ambulance screamed past, rounding the corner to the ER entrance. His chest tightened, the sound blending with memories of distant gunfire, explosions, and chaos. The beeping of medical equipment in his mind grew louder, and he closed his eyes, wishing the silence to return.

When he opened his eyes, he was back—at another hospital ...

Ethan blinked slowly, the effects of the anesthesia still lingering in his system. Lying in a hospital bed, a persistent throb in his arm reminded him of the bullet they'd dug out—a souvenir from a battle he'd rather forget.

A soft knock on the door frame snapped Ethan from his haze. He looked up to see Private Thompson limping into the room.

"Sarge, you hangin' in there?"

"Still breathing," Ethan rasped, forcing a small smile. "The others?"

Thompson's gaze drifted downward. "Carter ... Ramirez ... Davis. They didn't make it."

Ethan closed his eyes as his fingers clawed at the bedsheet, twisting the fabric. The air rushed from his lungs as if he'd been punched in the gut. Despite the spinning disorientation, his faculties wouldn't abandon him. Instead, his mind drifted to a newscast he heard before they had deployed.

"We're winning the war on every front," the politician had said.

Just not today …

No, today Ethan learned the truth: War isn't something you win—it's something you survive. And more than anything now, he hated it. Not because it was hard, but because the price of war is paid in lives. What victory could ever be worth that?

"But everyone else made it, Sarge. Thanks to you. What you did out there—you saved our lives."

Ethan's eyes fluttered open, red-rimmed and glistening. He swallowed hard. "Carter's wife … she's due next month. And Ramirez—" He had to fight to keep his voice steady. "—His little girl won't even remember him. And Davis … kid was barely old enough to drink." On the last word his voice broke, and he turned his face away from his brother-in-arms.

"You did everything you could, Sarge. We all did. And because of you, most of us are going home."

Ethan took a deep, shaky breath, trying to reconcile the loss with the lives saved. "It wasn't enough."

After what felt like an eternity, Ethan turned back to Thompson. "But we'll make sure they're never forgotten."

"We will." Thompson paused. "They were Rangers through and through. Rangers lead the way, right?"

Ethan nodded with a bittersweet smile, grateful for Thompson's words. "Always."

"Sarge, there's something else," Thompson said. "Some

dog followed us back to base."

Ethan's eyebrows shot up. "The dog, the Aussie Shepherd?"

"Yeah? He won't stop hanging around."

"Good. That dog saved my life. He came out of nowhere and started barking at me, and when I went over to see what was wrong, I had just missed the RPG explosion. If it hadn't been for him—"

Thompson's eyes widened. "Wait, you're serious?"

"Completely!"

"Sarge, if you want, we can look after him for you. It's the least we can do, considering what he did for you—for all of us, really."

"You'd do that? I-I don't even know what to say."

"Of course, Sarge. That dog's one of us now," Thompson said with a slight smile. "You know, we should probably give him a name. Can't keep calling him 'the dog' forever."

"You're right."

Silence fell between them. Then, almost simultaneously, they looked at each other.

"Hero," Ethan said.

Thompson smiled. "Perfect. Hero it is, then. Don't worry, Sarge. We'll take good care of him until you're back on your feet."

As they spoke, Ethan reached into his breast pocket and pulled out the worn Polaroid photo. The corners were tattered, but the image remained clear.

Thompson looked down at the photo. "That's your girl, Sarge?"

"Oh, um—"

SCREECH.

Ethan blinked again. The sharp sound of tires skidding along the pavement brought him back to reality. The car had barely stopped when its door flew open, and a woman launched herself out, racing toward the entrance.

His gaze traced the frantic movement of her coat, billowing behind her like wings as she ran. There was something about her movement, her silhouette, that kept his eyes glued to her.

Time seemed to slow as he took in every detail. Her tall, slender frame. The chestnut hair escaping its messy ponytail, whipping around her face. Those soulful brown eyes, wide with panic. The perfect curve of her lips, now pressed into a thin line.

Wait ... no.

But in a thousand different lives, her face was one he'd never forget.

As she got closer, a chill shot through Ethan's body ... His heart hammered against his ribs ... His limbs felt like lead.

What's she doing here?

5

Kara

"I NEED TO SEE her!" Kara blurted out, breathless, as she reached the receptionist's desk.

"Ma'am, may I ask who you are here to—"

"My daughter, Charlotte Walker—she's been in an accident!"

The receptionist nodded, fingers flying over the keyboard. "Do you know when she was—"

"Look, I just got a call. She's here somewhere. Please, which room?" Kara's words tumbled out as her fingers drummed on the desk.

"Of course, ma'am," the woman said, typing. "Room 237, second floor. Elevators are down the hall on the left."

"Thank you." She hurried around the desk and toward the elevators.

Kara pressed the button, waiting for the doors to part, but nothing happened.

She pressed it harder.

Still nothing.

"Come on," she muttered through gritted teeth, jabbing the button.

It sat on three.

Kara's gaze swept over the hallway. Spotting the stairwell sign, she darted through the door and raced up, two steps at a time, until she reached the second floor.

Once she emerged from the stairwell, she darted down the hall. *234, 235, 236 ...* The door to 237 stood open.

Kara looked at the first bed as she slipped inside. "Charlotte?"

But it was empty.

A sheet divided the room, the second half out of sight but not out of mind. Her chest tightened. She swallowed hard—and drew the sheet back.

"Mom?"

"Charlotte!" Kara closed the distance between them. "What happened? Are you all right?"

"Mom, breathe. I'm okay." Charlotte smiled. "Just a few scrapes and bruises."

"And your cheek." Kara reached out and touched Charlotte's chin.

"Courtesy of the five-star safety airbag. Right to the face. Not exactly the big soft balloon you'd imagine. They hit harder than you'd think."

"They barely told me anything on the phone, I—" Kara's vision blurred with unshed tears. "Are you sure you're all right, honey?"

"I am, Mom. Really."

"Well, what happened?"

"It was a deer. Out of nowhere. I swerved, then—a tree. Things got fuzzy after that, but I'm pretty sure the car is totaled." Charlotte's lips quirked into a half-smile. "And hey, no concussion. That's a win, right?"

Kara sighed, sinking into the plastic chair next to the bed. "What did the doctor say, honey? Shouldn't they be here?"

"Mom, seriously, they were just here," Charlotte said, reaching over and squeezing Kara's hand. "No need for the panic face, okay? They did x-rays and everything."

Knock. Knock.

The sheet rustled as a man stepped into view, his white jacket crisp, and his grayish-white hair neatly combed. "Ah, you must be Ms. Walker."

Kara pushed herself up, her fingers brushing across her cheeks, leaving damp trails on her skin. "Yes. Hello."

"I'm Dr. Samuels," he said. "I've been taking care of Charlotte since she was admitted. Her x-rays came back clear—no fractures."

"Does she need to stay overnight, just in case?"

"Not that I can see, and I don't think there's any reason to keep you here much longer either," he said. "I'll ask the nurse to bring in your discharge papers, and then you folks can get on home."

Kara hesitated. "Are you sure? No other tests or—"

"Mom," Charlotte groaned, her head falling back against the pillow. "The doctor literally just said I'm fine. Can we just trust the guy with the medical degree?"

Dr. Samuels chuckled. "Oh, that's all right. You're not the first worried parent to set foot in this hospital. Now, before I tell the nurse to get those papers, is there anything else I can answer for you?"

Kara glanced at Charlotte, then back at the doctor. "Yes—I mean, no. The only questions left are for my daughter. Thank you, Doctor."

"Wonderful. It was nice meeting you, Charlotte. You too, Ms. Walker." With a final nod, Dr. Samuels gave them both a reassuring smile before turning and quietly exiting the room.

As the door clicked shut behind him, Charlotte swung her legs off the bed. "See? All good. Hey, can you grab my clothes? They're in that bag over there. By my purse."

"Where were you when it happened?" Kara asked, grabbing the bag. She pulled out a wadded-up pair of jeans and handed them to her daughter.

"Not far from home," Charlotte mumbled, struggling to pull her jeans on under the gown. "By some old house, I think? But ... there was definitely a guy there. And—this is gonna sound weird—I'm pretty sure I heard a dog barking."

"A man and a dog? How'd you get here?"

"Yeah, and I think he's the one who called 911."

"Charlotte Walker?" A nurse walked into the room with a clipboard in her hands. "I have your discharge papers right here. Sign on this page, and you'll be free to go."

Charlotte grabbed the clipboard and signed her name at the bottom. "Here ya go."

Kara walked over, her mind momentarily drifting from the man and the dog.

"You'll need to take this to reception on your way out." The nurse handed them to Kara. "They'll finalize everything. And please call us if you experience any discomfort,

Charlotte."

Kara reviewed the papers, then looked up at the nurse. "Could I get the number to call, just in case?"

Charlotte tossed her hands up in the air. "Mom. Are you for real? The doctor said I'm fine!"

"All right, all right, but you—right, let's get going." Kara tucked the papers under her arm, then helped Charlotte gather her things. They made their way out of the room and toward the hospital exit.

As they approached the reception desk, Kara handed the discharge papers to the receptionist, who took them and began processing the final paperwork.

"Excuse me," the receptionist said, addressing Kara. "A man with a dog came by earlier asking about Charlotte. He said he wasn't family, so I didn't tell him what room she was in. I just wanted to let you know." She hesitated, then added, "Would you like me to call security to escort you to your car?"

"No, that's all right. We'll be fine. Thank you for letting us know, though."

The receptionist didn't seem convinced. She moved out from behind the desk and into the lobby. "Let me go with you to check if he's still around."

Kara hesitated, then nodded, deciding it was better to be safe.

As the three of them stepped outside into the warm evening air, the receptionist scanned the area.

"There," she said, pointing. "That's him, getting into that truck."

Kara squinted into the dimly lit parking lot, craning her

neck to follow the receptionist's outstretched finger. The man was too far away to see clearly, but that truck ...

A jolt surged through Kara's body, but she forced herself to breathe deeply, pushing the thoughts away.

No. Don't go there, Kara.

Kara shook her head and turned to the receptionist. "Thanks for your concern. We'll be fine from here."

Lots of people have blue Chevy trucks.

But as she helped Charlotte into the car, a nagging sensation coiled in her stomach.

What if it was him?

Kara's head swiveled back toward the blue Chevy truck. She couldn't help but watch as it pulled out onto the main road, its engine rumbling into the distance. For a moment, it was as if she were eighteen again, sitting in that same truck, the ocean breeze in her hair. Ethan's voice filling her ears and echoing through her mind, "I love you. You know that, right? I'll love you forever, Kara."

Why didn't he call?

Did he ever really love me?

Would he want to know about ...

The cool metal of the car door handle grounded her, pulling her back from memory lane into the present.

Stop. Focus on Charlotte. She needs you right now.

Kara took a long, steadying breath, her shoulders rising and falling as she willed Ethan's image to fade from her mind.

It couldn't have been him.

No way at all.

6

Ethan

ETHAN SLAMMED HIS FIST into the steering wheel, the vibration rattling his truck. He had seen the horrors of war and the worst of humanity. He'd saved his men from certain death in Afghanistan, even with a bullet lodged in his arm. But the sight of Kara after all these years? That sent him running like a coward.

She was right there.

Hero nudged Ethan's arm with his nose.

Ethan's throat tightened, but he reached over and scratched Hero behind the ears. "I'm all right, buddy."

Rubbing his throbbing temples, Ethan dragged himself out of the truck, and Hero followed him up the creaking porch steps of his dad's house. When he opened the front door, Hero sauntered in, nails clicking on the floor. Ethan followed, his muscle memory leading him through the dim house to the kitchen. He sat at the same table where he used to eat cereal before school and TV dinners alone at night.

Hero whined softly at his feet as Ethan's stomach growled. He hadn't eaten since leaving Virginia this morning. A TV dinner would feel like a feast right about now.

Guess some things never change.

He stood, then walked to the freezer. A blast of cold air hit his face as he yanked it open.

No luck.

The fridge wasn't any better. His eyes spotted the same jar of pickles from earlier. He reached for it and checked the label, then shook his head—expired.

I'll get food in the morning.

As he was about to close the door, he paused.

Wait—No beer?

His dad always packed the fridge with beer. Drank a six-pack every night. Maybe even finished the last one right before he ...

Sighing, Ethan shut the fridge and looked at Hero, who began lapping water from the pot he'd set to catch the leaky ceiling's drips.

"Hero, no." He gently tugged the dog away from the pot, wincing as water sloshed over the rim. After dumping it into the sink, he placed the pot back on the counter. "Stay put, all right? Got your stuff in the truck."

He headed to the truck and grabbed Hero's bag of supplies along with his own. Back inside, he dropped his bags by the door and unpacked Hero's supplies on the kitchen counter.

The dog watched him, tail swishing.

"You're the lucky one," Ethan said as he filled Hero's food bowl and set it down. "You get dinner tonight."

Hero immediately dug into his food, while Ethan filled a water bowl and placed it beside the food.

Ethan then opened a cupboard, searching for a clean glass. He found one, sort of. A film of dust coated its surface. With a sigh, he ran it under the tap, wiping it clean with his thumb before filling it with water. He was about to take a sip when—

Right, meds.

He placed the glass on the table and walked into the living room, which was dark and filled with the shadowy shapes of furniture he once knew well. Unzipping the side pocket of his bag, he fished out the familiar orange bottle, its rattle a reminder of the battles he still fought.

Back in the kitchen, he shook a pill into his palm and swallowed it dry only to wash it down with a gulp of water. The routine was so ingrained now, he barely thought about it anymore. But tonight, in this house full of memories, the act felt heavier somehow.

As he set the glass down, his phone buzzed in his pocket. He pulled it out and set it on the table, pressing speaker when he saw the voicemail.

"Mr. Bennett, Steve Clark here—your father's attorney." The voice crackled through the speaker. "Look, I hate to do this over voicemail, but we've hit a snag. Seems we're missing your father's house deed."

Ethan froze.

What's he talking about?

He'd spoken with Mr. Clark's office just last week. Everything should've been handled by now.

"I realize this complicates your plans to sell—no deed,

no sale. You'll need to check if your father stored it somewhere at home. If we can't locate it, we'll have to go through probate, the county recorder's office, and so on. Best case, we're looking at six to twelve months. Worst case? One to two years if the process drags."

Ethan's thoughts spiraled as the voicemail continued.

"Our office will be staying open later until about four tomorrow if you find anything. Call me when you can, and we'll figure this out."

The lawyer's voice faded, replaced by a resounding *BEEP!*

His father had never been the organized type, but the deed to the house? That was another level of carelessness.

Hero trotted over, pressing his head against Ethan's leg, and Ethan absentmindedly patted him.

It's gotta be here somewhere.

Leaning back against the sink, Ethan scanned the cluttered kitchen—dust clinging to shelves, drawers crammed with junk, and a pile of unopened mail spilling from a wicker basket. He rifled through the mail—no deed, just old bills and junk from the past year. He tossed them back into the basket, then sat back down and buried his face in his hands.

Ethan figured he'd come down from Virginia, tie things up with the house, and be done in a few days—maybe a week, tops. But who knew how long it'd take to find that deed?

He didn't want to be here.

Kara's face flashed in his mind.

His chest tightened, breath coming in shallow, uneven bursts at the thought of seeing her again.

He wasn't ready to face her.

Not after the way he left all those years ago. She probably hated him. She'd likely moved on by now, too.

He shook the thought away.

The deed. That's what he needed to focus on.

But not tonight.

As he stood, drinking the last of his water, he realized the house had gone eerily quiet.

"Hero." His voice echoed through the empty house. "Where'd you go, boy?"

He scanned the kitchen, then went into the hall.

Ethan searched the living room and den, but Hero was nowhere in sight. His pulse quickened as he checked the bedrooms and bathroom.

"Hero? Hero!"

He rushed down the hall and back to the kitchen.

Catching his breath, Ethan's gaze landed on the back door.

He blinked, rubbing his eyes as a small flap swayed at the base of the door. He crouched down, tracing its worn rubber edges—a doggy door. That hadn't been there when he lived here.

Standing, he turned the back door's rusty lock and pushed it open. Near it, he flipped the switch, and the porch light flickered on, casting a pale yellow glow over the yard. He let out a sigh as he saw Hero standing in the middle, sniffing at a patch of grass.

As he stepped out onto the small porch and climbed down the back steps, his eyes darted to the chain-link fence encircling the yard. That hadn't been there either.

A doggy door and a fenced yard ...

Since when did he have a dog?

Ethan's mind drifted to when he was ten, standing in front of his dad, holding the stray he'd found wandering the baseball field. "Please, Dad. He needs a home. I named him Wrigley."

His dad's bloodshot eyes had narrowed, hand gripping a half-empty bottle. "We can't take care of no stupid dog. Ain't got no means of feeding it," he'd slurred, forcing Ethan to turn the animal away.

The memory dissolved.

Ethan whistled. "Hero!"

He clapped his hands, and Hero came bounding toward him.

"Good boy," Ethan said, guiding Hero back inside. He knelt beside Hero, threading his fingers through the soft fur.

Hero licked his face, and for the first time all day, Ethan let himself smile. Hero didn't care about lost deeds or complicated pasts—he just wanted to be there, to offer comfort in his own quiet way.

"I know this isn't home, boy," he whispered. "But we won't be here long."

7

Kara

Saturday

BEADS OF SWEAT TRICKLED down Kara's temples, leaving salty streaks on her flushed cheeks as she finished taking the animals outside at the rescue. A short walk across the lush, dew-kissed lawn brought her to her tiny house.

When Kara opened the door, a soft voice floated from the kitchen. "Morning."

She hung her bag on a hook by the door and turned to find Charlotte rubbing her eyes. "How are you feeling?"

Charlotte winced as she rolled her shoulders. "Sore. A little groggy. But I think I'll survive."

Kara joined her at the table. "Need another aspirin?"

"Yeah, probably," Charlotte said, rising.

Before Charlotte could get up, Kara was in motion, her maternal instincts carrying her swiftly to the bathroom, where she retrieved the familiar white bottle from behind the mirrored cabinet door.

Charlotte sighed as Kara returned and handed her the bottle. "I could have gotten that, Mom."

"I know you could have. But you need to rest today. And I'm making your fav."

"Chocolate chip pancakes!"

Kara grabbed the mixing bowl of pancake batter from the fridge and brought it to the stove. "You know it."

"You da best." Charlotte stood and hugged Kara, then inched past and started the coffeemaker. "Want some?"

"Sure." Kara smiled.

Knock. Knock. Knock.

"Who's that?" Charlotte asked.

"Don't know." Kara stepped away from the stove and opened the front door.

"Hello, Kara." Whitaker Walker breezed past her, his salt-and-pepper hair neatly combed. A crisp button-down and freshly ironed slacks peeked out from beneath his starched white coat, while his polished loafers squeaked against the floor.

Kara's eyebrows shot up. "Dad?" She trailed after him. "I didn't know you were stopping by."

Charlotte spun around. "Grandpa!" She set down the two coffee mugs in her hand and wrapped her arms around his tall, lean frame.

"Hello dear. Always wonderful seeing you," he said.

Kara plastered on a smile. "Staying for breakfast, Dad?"

"Just some coffee. I have to head to the pharmacy soon," he said, settling into a chair. His eyes lingered on Charlotte.

"Your cheek—what happened?"

Charlotte touched the bruise. "It's nothing really. Just a bump from the car accident last—"

"Accident?" Whitaker shot his daughter the death stare. "Kara, what is she talking about?"

"Nothing to worry about. Charlotte is in one piece, and after we left the hospital—"

Whitaker pushed back his chair abruptly. "The hospital? And you didn't think to call me?" His voice rose. "Kara, how many times do I have—"

Charlotte stepped between them. "Here, Grandpa, just how you like it." She pressed the mug into his hands. "I even added the cream."

"Thank you, dear," he said, patting Charlotte's hand. Whitaker's gaze shifted to Kara. "You shouldn't have let her drive in the rain at night. You know how dangerous these roads can be."

Kara's stomach clenched as the memory of her mother's accident flashed through her mind—the call, the news, the helplessness. But she quickly refocused.

"Dad, are you sure you don't want pancakes?" she asked, pushing down the rising lump in her throat.

He shook his head. "I said coffee will do."

Kara pressed herself against the counter, her posture rigid as Charlotte maneuvered around her—a silent ballet they had mastered over the years.

"Don't you think this place is too small for two grown women?" Her dad took a slow sip of his coffee. "I still can't believe you sold the old house. I hope your petting zoo was worth it."

"Animal rescue, Dad," Kara said, biting her lip. She turned off the stove, then picked up a plate of chocolate-chip pancakes and carried it to the table. "This house is fine. And Charlotte is off at school most of the time now."

Charlotte squeezed into a chair. "I like this house."

"It's too cramped." Whitaker shook his head. "No Walker should live like this."

"Some might call it cozy," Kara said, forcing a smile as she reached for a towel, pretending to straighten things that didn't need fixing, anything to stay out of his line of fire. "You should drink up, Dad. I need to head out soon—gotta set up for the adoption event."

"Me too," Charlotte said, pouring syrup on her plate.

"No, you're not." Kara grabbed a stool and pulled it over to the table. "You're gonna stay here and rest."

"Mom ..."

"I'll have to agree with your mother, Charlotte," Whitaker said. "You should rest."

Charlotte straightened and turned to face her mom. "The doctor said I'm good. I'm helping you at the event today. Besides, if I'm there, you'll be able to keep an eye on me."

Kara sighed. "Okay. But as soon as you look the least bit tired, I'm sending you home."

Charlotte took a moment to finish her mouthful, then wiped her lips with a napkin. "Deal."

Kara's eyes flitted around the room, focusing on the chipped paint by the window, the stack of mail on the counter—anywhere but her father's face.

"Well girls, I'm heading off to the family pharmacy—one that, quite frankly, should be yours, Kara. But I suppose it will eventually fall to someone else." He stood, pushing the chair back under the table. "I'm glad you're home, Charlotte." He kissed the top of his granddaughter's head, then turned to his daughter.

"Kara." He put a hand on her shoulder. "We'll talk later."

"Bye Dad." Kara smiled at him, clenching her teeth. "Have a good day."

Walking out, his footsteps seemed to echo the distance Kara felt between them, a reminder of the years she had spent feeling overshadowed by his expectations. The old wounds, somehow, felt as raw as ever.

As soon as the door shut, Kara finally sat down, letting out a breath. She cut into her pancakes, eating in hurried bites between quick sips of coffee. "Charlotte, are you sure about coming to the rescue today? It won't be a big deal if—"

"I'm gonna hop in the shower and get dressed, then I'll be over." Charlotte stood, taking her plate to the sink. "Don't wait on me. I know you've got a ton to do this morning."

Kara swallowed the last bite of pancake, gulped her coffee in one long sip, and pushed back from the table. Her daughter was right—Kara did have a ton to do.

In the short distance from her house to the rescue, Kara's mind raced with the tasks ahead. As she unlocked the back entrance, a cheerful voice interrupted her thoughts.

"Hey, girl! Brought some drinks."

Kara turned to see Emma entering the yard, cooler in hand.

"Drinks, huh?" Kara raised an eyebrow with a smirk

Emma grinned. "Just water today. But if you're looking

for a real pick-me-up, I may or may not have some espresso shots stashed away. Anyway, I'm here to help. But first, how are you?"

The smile slid off Kara's face. "Well, my dad was here this morning. You know how that goes. And Charlotte was in a wreck last night. She's okay, but wants to help today, so we'll need to look out for her."

Emma set the cooler down. "Glad she's okay. Why didn't you tell me?"

"It was late. Didn't want to be a bother."

Emma stepped closer and grabbed both of Kara's shoulders, turning her friend to face her directly. "You're never a bother, no matter the time. Okay?"

"If you say so."

"I do say so. Now, did you find any more help for today?"

Kara shook her head. "No, it's only us and Charlotte. We'll manage."

Emma nodded. "Got it. Well, let's get started."

Kara nodded, then glanced around. "Oh, what about the volunteer booth? I completely forgot about it with everything going on."

"Don't you worry about that. I took care of it, just like I promised. Come on, I'll show you."

She led Kara to a corner of the lawn where a tent was already set up. A banner reading *Volunteer Information* hung across the front, and a table underneath was neatly arranged with clipboards, pens, and colorful flyers.

"Emma, this is amazing," Kara breathed, taking in the professional setup. "When'd you do all this?"

"I pulled up just as you were heading into your house

earlier from the rescue. Figured I'd get this done while you had a breather."

"You're a ninja and a lifesaver, truly."

"That's what friends are for. Now, let's get the rest of this place ready for some adoptions."

"Let's do it."

Kara and Emma fell into a rhythm, their movements a blur of efficiency as they transformed the space into an organized adoption venue. Tent poles clattered as they snapped into place, tables scraped across the ground as they were positioned, and the metallic clangs of cages and enclosures filled the air.

Charlotte arrived, greeting Emma with a warm hug. "Hey, Emma!"

"I heard about your wreck. You okay?"

Charlotte smirked. "Oh, you know me. I live on the dangerous side."

The trio burst into laughter, Kara shaking her head.

With everything in place, they began bringing out the animals. Leashes jingled and paws pattered as dogs were led to their designated spots. One by one, they placed the animals in enclosures or cages, each labeled with a name.

Kara did a final check, ensuring water dishes were full and blankets were comfortable in each cage. As she passed the one with Benny's name card, she stopped short. It was empty.

"Hey," she called out. "Has anyone seen Benny?"

Like clockwork, Charlotte strode in with Benny in tow, going at a slightly slower pace than the other dogs.

"There's my Benny," Kara said, walking over and bending

down to scratch behind his ears. "How are you doing today, buddy?"

Benny's soft brown eyes darted from person to person, his ears perked forward as he absorbed the flurry of activity around him.

Charlotte joined Kara, crouching beside her. "He's got beautiful eyes, don't you think?"

"Mm-hmm," Kara agreed with a smile, her gaze fixed on Benny. "He's a handsome boy, and I'm sure someone will see that today. Maybe today's the day you find your forever home. What do you think, Benny?"

Benny responded with a resounding bark as Charlotte and Kara stood back up.

Kara took a step back, her eyes marveling at the scene before her. The white tents, their fabric slightly muted under the overcast sky, formed a soft contrast against the grayish clouds. Rows of cages, their metal bars cool and reflective in the subdued light, were arranged meticulously along the lawn. Colorful adoption posters fluttered gently in the breeze, adding a touch of brightness to the surroundings. A small smile touched her lips as she thought of the new lives they might change today.

Turning to her friend and daughter, Kara's expression softened. "Thank you both so much for all your help. Couldn't have done this without you."

"We do make a pretty good team," Emma said, folding her arms.

Charlotte grinned, striking a superhero pose. "Yeah, we're like the Avengers of animal rescue."

Kara chuckled. "I always thought we were pretty amazing, but now it's official."

Just then, the first rays of sunlight broke through the clouds.

"Look," Emma said, pointing toward the entrance. "I think we've got our first visitors."

8

Ethan

ETHAN LAY THERE, FIGHTING off the pull of sleep, while feeling every ache from the lumpy mattress that had molded to his body overnight. He longed for the cloud-like comfort of his own bed but let himself enjoy a few more moments of rest.

However, Hero, ever the early riser, had other ideas. A warm tongue swiped across Ethan's cheek, leaving behind a trail of slobber.

"Morning, boy," he mumbled, scratching the dog's head.

With a soft whine and a gentle nudge of his cold nose, Hero made his intentions clear.

Ethan yawned, glancing at Hero's expectant face. "Gotta go out, huh? Go on then, you know the way."

Hero barked once and trotted out of the room. Ethan smiled, listening to the familiar click of Hero's nails against the floor as he made his way to the kitchen and out the doggy door. The doggy door was proving to be quite handy—now, if only Hero could figure out that he didn't need to wake Ethan for permission to use it.

Ethan stretched, shaking off the last traces of sleep, and headed to the bathroom for a quick shower. Once he was dressed in a fresh pair of worn jeans and a faded t-shirt faintly smelling of laundry detergent, he felt more like himself.

Today's objective: Find that deed.

If he found the deed by two or three, he could swing by the attorney's office and settle things by the end of the day. But just thinking about rummaging through dusty boxes and old filing cabinets made Ethan's head throb.

Correction, today's first objective: food.

Just then, Ethan heard the click of the doggy door, followed by the soft patter of paws on the kitchen floor. Hero appeared in the doorway, tail wagging, a stick clamped between his teeth.

Ethan couldn't help but grin at the dog's antics. "You know I'm useless without my coffee. Breakfast first, then we'll play."

***

Ethan and Hero headed out the front door and over toward the truck. As Ethan fished his keys from his pocket, the crunch of gravel underfoot caught his attention. He looked up, squinting against the sunlight to see Clyde Jefferson, his old neighbor, still as spry as ever.

"Well, I'll be! Ethan? That you?"

"Yes, sir," Ethan called back, circling to the truck's rear.

"My, how you've grown." Clyde adjusted his glasses with

a broad smile, looking down. "And who's this handsome fella?"

Ethan patted Hero's head. "This is Hero. My partner in crime."

"Nothing beats a good dog," Clyde nodded, then winced, rubbing his elbow. "Say, I hate to ask, but my arthritis is acting up. Mind helping an old man with his groceries?"

"Not at all. Just lead the way, sir."

"Still polite as ever, but no need for 'sir,'" Clyde said with a chuckle. "Just 'Clyde' will do."

Ethan grinned as he walked to the next driveway, Hero in tow. "Of course, Clyde."

Clyde opened his trunk and stepped back. "Good to see you back in town, though I'm sorry about what happened to your old man."

Ethan hefted a load of bags. "Yeah, it's a shame, but I won't be here for long. Just here until I sort things out with his place."

"Remember when you used to lend me a hand with the yard work?" Clyde shuffled toward the front door. "You were such a good kid. Always reliable."

"I can still help out if you need anything while I'm here."

"Oh, don't you worry." Clyde waved him off. "Already got someone helping these days. But I appreciate the thought."

As they stepped inside, the house felt as warm and welcoming as Ethan remembered. The air was infused with the comforting scent of cedarwood and citrus. Soft, golden light spilled from antique lamps in the corners. Plush, mismatched throw pillows adorned the overstuffed sofa. Family photos and artwork lined the walls. Among the personal touches, a rustic wooden sign hung, hand-painted with the words: *Home isn't always where you left it, but sometimes it's where you least expect to find it.* The space felt deeply lived-in and loved, and as Ethan took it all in, a quiet sense of peace settled over him.

Hero paused at the door with a whine.

Clyde's eyes flicked to Hero. "That four-legged friend of yours is welcome too, you know."

"Thanks," Ethan nodded, glancing at Hero. "He's my shadow—most of the time. Come on, boy."Hero bounded inside after the two.

"Just dump 'em on the kitchen table, if you don't mind."

Ethan returned his attention to Clyde, who now gestured down the hall, and as they entered the kitchen, Ethan's eyes and mind drifted to that kitchen table: late-night knocks, the comforting smell of coffee, and Clyde patiently listening to him talk about his dad's drinking. It was a safe place when he needed it the most.

"Thank you, Ethan," Clyde said as Ethan set down the groceries.

"You're very welcome, sir. I mean Clyde." Ethan saw a notepad on the table, jotted his number down on it, and slid it over to Clyde. "Here's my number. Like I said, I won't be here for long, but if you need any help, just call me."

Clyde's eyes crinkled with a smile as he walked Ethan to the door. "You're a good man, Ethan. Always have been." He paused, hand on the doorknob. "Say, before you skip town, how about we grab a cup of coffee? Catch up?"

Warmth spread through Ethan's chest. "Yeah, I'd like that. I'll swing by before I go."

Ethan's stomach growled as Hero settled into the passenger seat, pawing at the window. "All right, all right, I'll crack it open for you," Ethan said with a grin, rolling the window down a few inches as they pulled out of the driveway.

Once they hit the open road, Hero leaned into the breeze, ears flapping in the wind. His tail thumped against the seat, keeping time with the whoosh of passing cars as the briny air from the coast filled the truck. The road stretched ahead, and Ethan wondered if his old go-to spot for a good meal was still around after all these years. The drive passed quicker than he expected, the landscape both familiar and changed in subtle ways.

Turning onto Main Street was like stepping into a living postcard. The buildings stood proud in their coastal palette: cerulean blues like clear summer skies, soft buttery yellows that captured the warmth of sunrise, and weathered reds that echoed the fiery hues of sunset. The aroma of fresh-brewed coffee and the sweet spice of cinnamon rolls just out of the oven drifted from the corner bakery, mingling with the earthy scent of damp wood from the docks. Sun-baked rope and the ever-present undertone of the sea lingered in the air. By the time he reached the diner, its familiar sign came into view, standing just as he remembered.

Lucky me.

With Hero at his side, the familiar bell above the door jingled and heads turned as Ethan entered Phil's Diner. The lull in conversation picked back up in hushed tones as he went to an empty stool at the end of the counter. Still, he felt the eyes of the other patrons linger on his back.

What's their deal? Is this about Dad ... what he did? I guess in a town like this, people don't forget—even after twenty years.

"Ethan? Oh, Ethan?" A familiar, shrill voice cut through the diner. "Is that really you? I haven't seen you in ages!"

Ethan turned just in time to see an older woman coming up to him, her red glasses perched crookedly on the bridge of her nose, and wild, silver-streaked hair puffed out in every direction as if she'd just wrestled with the wind. He smiled at the familiar face. "Hey, Ada. Good to—"

Before he could say another word, Ada swooped in, wrapping him in a hug so tight he nearly lost his breath. An intense floral scent made Ethan's nose twitch. It was a cocktail of roses, lilies, and something sickeningly sweet. It clung to the air, just like Ada herself.

"Well, look at you. How long's it been? Oh, now wait a minute. Phil!" Ada's voice rang out, her arms still locked around Ethan in a surprisingly strong grip for her compact frame. "Phil! Get out here! You'll never guess who's back!"

Phil emerged from the kitchen, wiping his hands on his apron. His eyebrows shot up. "Ethan? Well, I'll be. How many years has it been?"

Ethan extended his hand, grasping Phil's firmly, feeling the calluses and strength in the older man's grip. "Far too many."

"And who's this?" Phil asked, bending down, hand outstretched.

"This is Hero," Ethan said, watching the interaction.

Ada bent down, patting Hero's head. "What a handsome

boy," she said with a smile, then reached into her purse, rummaging around. "Let me see if I've got a little treat for you ..."

Her hand came up empty, and she frowned. "Oh, shoot. Thought I had a snack in here for you." She gave Hero an apologetic look. His tail, which had started wagging, now drooped.

"He's not picky, but looks like you're off the hook this time." Ethan chuckled, then turned to Phil. "He usually goes where I go. Hope it's all right I brought him in?"

"Course it's all right!" Phil said, bringing Ethan's attention back to him with his boisterous voice. "So, where've you been hiding all these years?"

"Virginia. Been there a while now."

"Well, welcome home!" Phil said, clapping him on the back. "Say, I remember reading about you. Silver Star from Afghanistan, wasn't it?" He shook his head in amazement. "A bona fide hero right here in my diner. Who'd have thought?"

Ethan's hand found the back of his neck, his gaze dropping to Hero. "It's ... not as big a deal as it sounds. Lot of guys got 'em."

Ada swatted Ethan's arm. "Oh, stop being so modest! You're a genuine hero, Ethan. Own it!"

Ethan forced a smile, his thoughts drifting to the men he'd saved—and those he hadn't. "Thanks."

Ada's eyes sparkled as she squeezed his bicep. "My goodness! These are the real deal. Why don't they cast real heroes in those military movies? Wouldn't need all that fancy camera work."

Ethan chuckled, trying to ease his arm away. "You're too kind, Ada. Really."

Ada's grip tightened, her voice dropping to a conspiratorial whisper. "I mean it, Ethan. Take that guy who played the military hero in that movie—what was his name? ... Doesn't matter. He looked like he'd never seen a push-up in his life, much less done one." She gave his arm another affectionate squeeze.

Phil, observing with an amused grin, cleared his throat. "All right, Ada. Let's not scare the poor boy off. We want him to actually come back, you know."

Ada turned to Phil, her lower lip jutting out in an exaggerated pout. "Oh, you're no fun." She released Ethan's arm with a dramatic sigh. "Fine, fine. I'll behave."

"Now Ethan, how long are ya sticking around?"

"Longer than I'd hoped." Ethan let out a dry chuckle. "Hoping to tie things up in a week or so."

Phil turned to Ethan. "I see, well at least I can feed you while you're here. So, what'll it be? Name it, and it's yours. On the house, of course."

Ethan shifted on his stool. "I appreciate it, but you don't have to do that."

"I won't hear of it. Now, what can I get ya?"

Ethan's eyes skimmed the menu. "All right, if you insist. How about hash browns, toast, some OJ, and a cup of coffee?"

"Coming right up," Phil nodded, then glanced at Hero. "And don't worry, I've got something special for your four-legged friend too." With that, he disappeared into the kitchen.

Ada slid onto the stool next to Ethan, leaning in so close he could smell her floral perfume mixing with coffee and pancakes. "So, what's on the agenda while you're here? Any exciting plans for today?"

"Just working on my dad's house, really," Ethan said. "Like I said, I'm not staying long."

Ada's nose wrinkled. "Well, that sounds dreadfully dull. Say, why don't you come by the animal rescue's adoption day? Might liven things up a bit."

Animal rescue?

Ethan refocused on Ada. "Actually, I used to work at a rescue back in Virginia. It was—"

"Wonderful! We'll go together. I'll be your personal tour guide."

"But …" Memories of the animal rescue in Virginia flooded back. Since an animal had saved his life, he figured he'd repay the favor; so, after he retired from the Army two years ago, he started volunteering at a local rescue to eat up time. Turned out he loved every minute. He'd thrown himself into the work, learning everything he could about animal care and behavior. It had become his passion, and the rescue had become like a second home, the staff and volunteers like family. But then, just a few months ago, the rescue had closed down because of lack of funding. It had been a gut punch, leaving Ethan feeling adrift once again. He'd lost not just a job, but a community, a sense of purpose.

Shaking off the bittersweet memories, Ethan's fingers drummed on the counter. His gaze flickered between Ada's hopeful face and the clock on the wall. "You know what? Maybe I'll stop by. Just for a little while."

Ada grinned. "Then it's a date. We can ride over together."

"Uh, I've got Hero with me, and I really need to get back to the house after. I don't think—"

"Nonsense!" She swatted his arm. "Hero can come too. You can drive us."

Ethan glanced up at the small window to the kitchen to see Phil laughing.

"All right Ada. We'll all go together," Ethan said accepting his fate. Saying "no" to Ada Harrison was like trying to stop a freight train with a feather.

Phil came out with a loaded plate of food—wisps of heat drifting up—and set it down in front of Ethan with a soft clatter. The plate was piled high with crispy golden hash browns, perfectly toasted bread, and a small dish of assorted jams. He followed it up with a steaming cup of coffee, setting it beside a tall glass of fresh-squeezed orange juice.

"Here ya go," Phil said with a wink. Then he reached into his apron pocket and pulled out a small bag. "And for Hero ..."

Crouching, Phil scattered a few treats near Hero's paws. The dog's tail became a blur of motion as he investigated the unexpected bounty.

Phil straightened with a grunt. "They're from Barking Orders. Started keeping 'em for our four-legged customers." He jerked a thumb towards Ada. "Got 'em from that rescue she was yapping about, actually."

Hero made quick work of the treats, looking up hopefully for more.

Phil chuckled. "Easy there, big fella. That's your lot for

now. Don't want to ruin your actual breakfast, do we?"

Ethan smiled, touched by Phil's thoughtfulness. "Thanks, Phil."

"Don't mention it. Now, better fuel up. Sounds like Ada's got quite the day planned for you."

As the aroma of his meal wafted up, Ethan dug in. Meanwhile, Ada's voice became a steady backdrop, prattling on about everything that had changed—and everything that hadn't—in Hadley Cove.

Ada bounced to her feet the moment Ethan's fork hit the empty plate. "Perfect timing! Ready to head out?"

"Sure, Ada." Ethan rose slowly, shooting Ada a pointed look. "Just remember, I won't be able to stay long. I've got lots to—"

"Oh, details, details," Ada said, flapping a dismissive hand. She steered him towards the door, patting his arm. "A couple of hours, tops. You'll hardly notice the time fly."

Ada darted forward with unexpected agility, her red glasses sliding down her nose with each quick step. Her silver hair bobbed as she practically dragged Ethan toward his truck. Suppressing a groan, Ethan followed her into the warm summer air, and Hero padded alongside them, oblivious to the fact that Ethan's day was now far from his own.

The short walk to the truck was filled with Ada's chatter. As they reached the vehicle, Ethan opened the passenger door with a smile, holding it for Ada. She climbed in with a small grunt, brushing off her floral-print blouse, her perfume wafting around him like a cloud. Hero leaped into the back seat, settling in.

Ethan shut the door and rounded the front to the driver's

side with a resigned sigh.

Ada ran a finger along the dashboard. "Well, well. This old beast is still kicking, huh?" Her gaze roamed over the weathered interior. "Ain't this the same truck from your wild days? I swear I can still hear you boys gunning the engine, thinking you were hot stuff."

The door's familiar groan as Ethan settled behind the wheel brought a flood of memories. He chuckled. "She's not pretty, but she gets me where I need to go."

Ada settled back, her eyes twinkling. "I can still see you boys tearing down Main Street like you were kings of the road." She patted the dash fondly. "Can't believe you've held onto her all this time. Some things stick with us, don't they?"

Ethan's fingers traced the steering wheel's worn grooves. "Yeah," he murmured, more to himself than Ada. "Some things stay with you forever."

Ada's finger jabbed at the windshield. "Hang a right at the end here, then your first left. Big signs everywhere—even you can't get lost."

He made a right turn, following Ada's directions. But when he was about to make a left, he realized he couldn't. The parking lot was full of people, large tents, food trucks, and all sorts of things going on. So, he pulled off to the side of the road and parked.

Ethan eyed the bustling street. "Looks like walking from here. Here, let me give you a hand."

Jumping down from the truck, he ran over to the other side and helped Ada out, then took Hero out of the back.

As they crossed the road, Hero's ears perked up at the

cacophony of barking and excited chatter. It was more like a fair than an adoption day.

Ethan looked up at the name painted in big letters across the entrance: *Second Chance Animal Rescue.* The perfect name for a place like this, or so he thought to himself.

Before he could take a few more steps, a familiar figure at the edge of his vision caught his attention. It was the young woman from the accident. *So, she is okay?*

The young woman's brow furrowed when he approached, a hint of recognition dawning in her eyes. "Hey, don't I know you?"

9

Kara

"Hey, Mom!" Kara felt a gentle tap on her shoulder and turned away from the table. Charlotte was standing there, her eyes gleaming. "I'd like you to meet someone."

Kara's gaze flickered to the man standing beside Charlotte, and her breath hitched.

"This is Ethan. He was there last night, called for help and everything. Crazy, right?" She crouched, her hand outstretched to the dog next to him. "Oh, and this beautiful boy is Hero! My Hero, yes you are, who's a good boy?"

Seeing him again felt like someone had shaken her awake from a long-forgotten dream.

Kara's heart pounded as she tried to make sense of it all—Ethan, standing there, as if the years hadn't passed. But they had. Twenty-two years, full of *what ifs* and *could've beens*.

"Oh ... hey," Kara managed, her voice barely above a whisper. Her eyes locked onto Ethan's, unable to look away as her hand blindly reached behind her, fumbling for a brochure on the table, fingers clenching around the paper, the glossy finish crinkling as she absorbed the sight of the unexpected duo before her.

"Kara," Ethan said.

His voice had a rumble that resonated through her. It was deeper than the memories she had of it, but it wasn't all that had changed. The lines around his eyes had deepened, and sandy blonde hair had given way to salt-and-pepper streaks. He'd also filled out, his shoulders broader than she remembered. But his stance, the way he held himself—that was all very familiar, achingly so.

As her gaze traveled lower, she noticed something new: intricate tattoos wound down his left arm, peeking from beneath his sleeve. Black ink patterns twisted around his bicep, the design full of symbols she couldn't quite make out, but their presence added a roughness to him that hadn't been there before. This Ethan was different, shaped by years she hadn't been a part of.

"It's just like in the movies, isn't it?" Charlotte bounced on her toes. "Mom, aren't you gonna thank him?"

Kara blinked, coming back to herself. "Right, yes. Thanks, Ethan. For helping Charlotte. If you hadn't ..." Her voice trailed off.

Ethan shrugged, looking uncomfortable with the praise. "Anyone would've done the same. Just luck that I was nearby."

"I'll say." Charlotte put her hands on her hips. "And here you are, showing up to the adoption event. What are the chances?"

Kara forced a faint smile and crossed her arms.

Charlotte glanced back and forth between them. "Well, I'm just glad we all got to meet."

Ethan's hand moved to the back of his neck. "Actually, we've—"

"Well, hello ladies!" Ada's voice broke in as she approached. "Kara, Charlotte, this is so wonderful! And is that a snow cone stand I spotted?"

Kara nodded, grateful for the interruption. "Good eye, Ada. Some folks from town volunteered to run it. All the proceeds go to the rescue."

Ada rummaged in her purse, retrieving a crisp paper check, which she handed over with a flourish. "I wanted to drop this off. And wouldn't you know, I bumped into Ethan here who offered me a ride."

Kara accepted the check, her mouth falling open at the figure staring back at her. "Ada, this is—wow. You have no idea how much this will help us."

Ada waved off Kara's surprise. "It's nothing, dear. I know you'll put it to good use." She adjusted the strap of her purse on her shoulder, glancing around with an approving nod. "Now, how's the event going? Good, I hope?"

Kara's professional demeanor returned as she surveyed the crowd. The scent of kettle corn drifted through the air from a nearby cart as laughter mixed with the occasional yip of a dog. Families meandered through the rows of animal pens, children tugging their parents toward the playful dogs. Couples strolled hand in hand, smiling at the animals and chatting as they paused to read adoption signs.

"It's been great, actually. Lots of visitors, and the animals are loving the attention. I think we might get a few adoptions today."

Charlotte leaned in, giving her mom a quick side hug. "Told you everything would come together. It's going even better than we planned."

Kara returned the hug, then gently disentangled herself from her daughter's embrace. Clearing her throat, she smoothed out the crumpled brochure in her hand. "Well, I should get back to—"

"Wait a minute." Ada blurted. "Weren't you two a thing? Way back when?"

Kara's spine snapped straight, the words hitting her like a cold gust of wind. Her gaze darted to Ethan, finding him suddenly fascinated with the ground, his hands shoved deep into his pockets.

Kara swallowed hard, knowing she'd have to field this one. "Well, Ada, we—"

From the corner of her eye, Kara caught a flash of movement.

"Ada, hey!" Emma rushed over, gently grasping Ada's wrist. "Sorry to interrupt, but I could really use your help with something. Charlotte too, if y'all are free?" She glanced at Kara. "It's a bit of a three-person job."

Ada hesitated, looking back at Kara and Ethan. "Oh, but we were in the middle of—"

"It'll just take a minute, promise," Emma insisted, already steering Ada away. She caught Kara's eye, a silent understanding passing between them. "We'll be right back!"

Kara let out a small sigh. *Thank you, Em.*

Charlotte didn't need to hear any more, not before Kara

could explain things to her.

"Oh, just one more thing!" Charlotte came running back, slightly out of breath. "Ethan, you should totally volunteer here sometime. The animals would love you! We also kinda really need the help."

"Thanks," Ethan said with a half-smile. "I'll, uh, think about it."

Charlotte snatched a brochure from her mom's hand and handed it to Ethan. "Here, take this. It's got all the info—the animals we help, how to sign up, shift times, everything. We're pretty flexible, and Mom's usually around to train new folks. You'd pick it up in no time!"

Kara froze, momentarily stunned. *What is she doing?*

Charlotte smiled at him, then gave her mom a knowing glance and a wink. "Okay, gonna help Emma now!" She ducked away and disappeared into the crowd, giving Hero one last scratch behind the ears.

Kara turned back to Ethan. What could she possibly say after all these years to the person she thought, once upon a time, that she'd spend her whole life with?

A lengthy silence stood between them before she said the only thing that came to mind. "Nice day, huh?"

The words hung in the air.

Kara mentally facepalmed herself. *Of all topics. The weather. Really?*

Ethan's head bobbed, seemingly unfazed by her best conversation starter. "Yeah, it's ... pleasant? Cooler than I expected for May."

Kara drew in a slow breath. This was her chance to redeem herself, a second chance rescue—if there ever was one—at a better first impression. She willed her voice to be steady. "So, when did you get back?"

"Just drove in yesterday," he said, patting Hero's head. "Dad passed, so I'm getting everything sorted. Probably heading back in a few days."

The awkwardness seemed to evaporate in the face of this news. "Oh, Ethan—I had no idea. I'm so sorry."

Ethan shrugged. "Thanks. It's—yeah." He paused. "I'm just relieved Charlotte wasn't hurt in that accident."

Kara's brow furrowed, thrown by the shift in conversation. "Wait, so why were you there?"

"It happened right in front of Dad's place." Ethan's gaze grew distant, unfocused for a moment. "Heard the crash and rushed out to it." His attention shifted back to the glossy paper in his hands as he flipped it over.

"Oh." Kara's eyes followed his and her stomach churned as memories of late-night edits and rushed printing flooded her mind. She bit her lower lip. The cheaper paper felt like a glaring mistake now.

"You don't have to read it all," Kara muttered, resisting the urge to snatch it back. "It's—not our best work. Threw it together last minute."

Ethan looked up, meeting her eyes. A small, reassuring smile lifted the corners of his mouth. "Are you kidding? This is incredible, Kara. The layout, the information—it's really well done. You should be proud of this."

Those ocean-blue eyes were just as deep and mesmerizing as they'd been twenty years ago when they sat in his old blue Chevy. For a split second, she was eighteen again, inside his truck with the scent of salt and the grit of sand clinging to her skin. His fingers entwined with hers one last time, promising to call. The bittersweet ache of leaving him, not knowing it would be the last time they'd be together like that. She remembered Ethan's words: "I love you. You know that, right? I'll love you forever, Kara." *But did he mean it? Does he still—*

The memory dissolved as Hero's soft whine pulled Kara back to the present. She shook her head, forcing herself to focus. Her eyes went to Hero, who had settled at Ethan's feet, his mismatched eyes calmly tracking the people and animals milling around them.

"Must have taken a lot of work to get it to this point. How long have you had this place?" Ethan's voice brought her attention back to him.

"Going on twenty years now," Kara said. "It was a slow start. Renovating the old barn alone took almost a year. But now?" She gestured around them. "We try to host these events monthly. I wish we could do more but, well, you can imagine the work involved."

"You're amazing, you know that?" His eyes swept over the area before landing back on Kara.

Kara's cheeks warmed under his gaze.

Amazing? After all this time, he still thinks I'm amazing?

She tucked a loose strand of hair behind her ear, buying time to compose herself. Part of her wanted to bask in the compliment, but another part remembered the pain of their separation and urged caution.He cleared his throat. "I mean, this is all amazing. I'm guessing you have a pretty big team of volunteers to pull off something like this?"

"We do. Well, sort of—used to. Could always use more

hands." Kara hesitated. "Look, about what Charlotte said. There's no pressure, okay? I know you're not staying long. It was just her being Charlotte."

Ethan's gaze locked onto hers, those gorgeous eyes appearing to see right through hers. "And if I wanted to volunteer? Would that be okay?"

The question lingered between them, loaded with two decades of unspoken words and missed opportunities.

Every second stretched impossibly long. She knew that whatever she said next could change everything—again.

Kara's heart hammered, her pulse drumming in her ears, as if the moment itself held its breath, waiting for the right words to fill the space, but what came out was, "Well, I mean if—"

10

Ethan

BEEP! BEEP! BEEP!

Ethan fumbled in his pocket, silencing the insistent alarm before sliding the phone back into his jeans. "Shoot. I gotta run." He waved the brochure. "This okay to take?"

Kara gave a small nod. "Of course, that's what they're for."

"Thanks. I'd love to stick around, but I can't be late." Ethan whistled, patting his leg. "Come on Hero. Time to head home, buddy."

As Ethan moved to leave, Kara's voice blew through the air, light and just as beautiful as his memory afforded her. "If you really want to help, feel free to stop by while you're in town. I'll be here tomorrow—and the next day. Pretty much every day." She chuckled, the sound soft, almost nervous, cute.

Her smile lingered, and Ethan's gaze caught on her eyes—deep brown, just as he remembered. There was something both familiar and different about them: traces of the girl he once knew, but now grounded in a quiet confidence earned through years of life. They were inviting, magnetic even, and Ethan felt a sudden reluctance to leave.

"Maybe I will. It was good seeing you again—Kara."

"You too." She gave him a polite, tight-lipped smile.

Ethan shifted his weight, offering a small smile of his own. "Maybe I'll see you around."

Kara raised her hand in a half-wave, her fingers barely moving, before turning on her heel and disappearing under the billowing tent.

Twenty minutes later, the crunch of gravel under his tires signaled Ethan's arrival at his dad's driveway. He stepped out, unlocked the door, and headed straight to the kitchen, Hero at his side. As he moved through the familiar space, his thoughts wandered back to Kara.

Does she have a partner? ... Who am I kidding? Of course she does. A woman like Kara doesn't stay single for long.

The idea of Kara's gentle hands intertwined with a faceless figure standing beside her ... on endless repeat. The thought—it stirred an ache in his chest, something deeper he couldn't quite name.

Ethan rubbed his temples, willing the unwanted thoughts to dissipate.

You don't get to wonder about that anymore. You gave up that right a long time ago.

As he cranked open the window above the sink, letting the crisp air rush in, an image of Charlotte flashed in his mind. The resemblance was uncanny—a mirror of Kara—tall, slender frame, and chestnut hair. Save one difference: Charlotte's eyes were blue.

Hero whined, a paw striking Ethan's thigh.

"You can go outside if you want," Ethan said, looking down at Hero. "I'll be an hour—you know the drill."

Hero let out a sharp bark before trotting out through the doggy door.

Ethan shook his head and stepped into the hallway, grabbed a backpack from the pile of bags, and returned to the kitchen table. Sitting down, he pulled out his laptop, set it in front of him, and switched on the hotspot from his phone. A few minutes later, he was logged in and ready for his weekly therapy session to begin.

Ethan glanced at the clock—two minutes past the scheduled start time. Still no sign of his psychiatrist.

He began scrolling through his calendar, double-checking that he had the correct day.

As he was about to send a message to confirm, the video call ringtone chimed from his laptop.

"Hey, Ethan. Sorry about the wait. I had a session that ran over." A middle-aged woman with kind eyes smiled at him.

Ethan let out a chuckle. "No problem. Glad I didn't screw up the time this week."

Dr. Hartman adjusted her glasses, her face inching closer to the camera. "This isn't your usual setup. Are you at home?"

"No, I'm at," Ethan said, glancing around. "I'm at my dad's place. In Hadley Cove."

"Of course, you mentioned this trip. How's it going so far?"

"It's been," Ethan rubbed his jaw, feeling the day-old stubble scratch against his palm, "a lot. Non-stop since I arrived yesterday."

"Walk me through it, Ethan. What's been going on?"

"Heh. Where do I even start?" Ethan exhaled slowly, his fingers drumming on the table. "I guess when I first got to the house ..."

As Ethan recounted the events, his eyes remained fixed on the computer screen. The psychiatrist's image occasionally froze for a split second before catching up, her head nodding in gentle encouragement. Occasionally, her gaze shifted slightly to the side, perhaps glancing at her notes or typing something into the computer out of view.

In the corner of the video feed, Ethan watched the call duration tick upward: ten minutes ... fifteen ... twenty ...

A slight crease appeared on Dr. Hartman's forehead as she listened, her posture unchanged except for the occasional shift in her chair.

A notification popped up on his screen: *Battery Low: 20% remaining.*

Ethan blinked, realizing how long he had been talking.

"And you just found out about this?" she asked. "About the missing deed?"

"Last night," Ethan said. "Anyway, I gotta find it soon."

"I see. It's got to be tough dealing with all of your late father's affairs."

"Wouldn't be so bad if it weren't for the deed. Thought I'd be back home in a few days. But now? I'm looking at a week, minimum. And if it doesn't turn up? The lawyer's talking about courts, legal proceedings." Ethan ran a hand through his hair. "Says it could drag on for years. I just—" He sighed, rolling his shoulders. "I need this over with to move on, you know?"

Dr. Hartman nodded. "I understand. I would be just as frustrated."

"Well, I'm not thrilled about it. And then last night, there was this accident." He shook his head.

"An accident? What happened?"

"This girl crashed into a tree on the side of the road. Right outside the house. The rain was terrible last night, but by some miracle, she wasn't badly injured."

"Sounds like she was very fortunate."

Ethan nodded. "Yeah, actually ran into her today. And then ... well, I saw someone else I knew."

Dr. Hartman raised a brow. "Really?"

Ethan sighed. "Yeah. Kara."

"Kara? As in *the* Kara we've discussed before?"

"Yeah, that Kara. Right before our session, I was grabbing something to eat in town. Ended up at this animal rescue event. And who do I see? Charlotte—the girl from the ac- cident—introducing me to her mom. And of all people, it's Kara."

"Small world. What do you think about all of this?"

Ethan laughed. "That I've forgotten what this town is like—everyone knows everyone, and everyone knows everyone's business too."

"And how was it talking with Kara again?"

"It was ..." Ethan thought back to the conversation. "Surreal. Her face went pale when she saw me. Can't blame her."

"What did you talk about?"

Ethan shrugged. "The animal rescue, mostly. Then her daughter suggested I volunteer there. Can you believe it?"

"Didn't you enjoy volunteering at the other animal rescue?"

"Yeah, but—" Ethan's head snapped up. "Wait, you think that's a good idea? I mean don't you think it seems like a lot?"

She studied Ethan's face. "Do you? If so, why? What's really stopping you?"

Ethan laughed. "Well, for starters we'd be working side by side, and I—What do you say to someone after all these years? And maybe it's too late for us, you know? Plus, I'll be gone soon once I find this deed. And—"

"Too late for what? Too late to pick up where you left off?"

Ethan shook his head. "No, no. That ship's long gone. At least I think it is, might be, I-I don't know. Maybe we could be friends? Is that crazy?"

"It's not crazy," she said. "Let me ask you something else. That animal rescue you worked at back home—have you found anything else that gives you that same sense of purpose?"

"No." Ethan slumped in his chair. "Nothing's come close since."

Dr. Hartman tapped her pen. "Maybe this is your chance to get back to something that fills your cup. I know Kara's presence might complicate things, but getting back to animal work could be beneficial, or it might be too much too soon. But you'll have to decide that for yourself."

Ethan chewed his lip, thinking it over. "I'll need some time to decide."

"Take your time," she said, leaning back. "And remember, if you decide to volunteer and need me in the middle of it all, I'm only a phone call away."

Ethan nodded. "Thanks, Doc. That means a lot."

She glanced at her computer screen. "Oh, before I forget—you're due for a medication refill. Want me to send it to a pharmacy in Hadley Cove?"

Ethan winced. "Yeah, that'd be great, just not Walker's though. Any other place works."

"No problem. I'll have my assistant call it in. You'll get a text later."

"Perfect, thanks."

"We've covered a lot today. Anything else on your mind before we wrap up?"

A scratching sound drew Ethan's attention to the doggy door. He smiled as Hero trotted in. "Nah, I think that's it for now. See you next week?"

"Absolutely."

With a soft click, Ethan shut his laptop and reached down to stroke Hero's fur.

"What do you think, boy? Should I volunteer at the rescue?" Hero woofed softly, then padded over to his water bowl. He pawed at it a couple of times before giving it a nudge, sending it toppling over and splashing water across the floor.

Ethan chuckled, shaking his head. "Nice move, Hero. So, is that a yes, or are you just dodging the question?"

11

Kara

Sunday

KARA DUNKED THE MOP into the bucket, the pungent smell of disinfectant rising with the splash of soapy water. Her muscles ached as she prompted the coarse bristles to scratch against the floor of another kennel.

Only eight more to go.

When she reached Benny's door, she paused.

His cloudy eyes blinked slowly as she crouched and reached through the bars, scratching under his salt-and-pepper beard.

Kara smiled softly. "Good morning, beautiful boy."

Standing back up, she rolled her shoulders to ease the stiffness. As she gripped the mop to continue, the door swung open, and Emma breezed in with a pink box of doughnuts in hand.

Kara blinked. "What are you doing here so early?"

"Checking in on you. Thought you could use a pick-me-up," she said, raising her voice over the chorus of excited barks as she set the doughnuts on a nearby shelf. "After yesterday's event, no adoptions, and then running into—"

"Ethan," Kara finished, her voice barely above a whisper, drowned out by the barks.

Emma studied Kara's face, waiting for the furry residents to calm back down. Finally, she asked, "How are you holding up?"

Kara leaned on her mop. "I—it's hard to process, you know? Twenty-two years, and then bam! He's right there in front of me."

"I can only imagine. Here, let me help." Emma gently pried the mop from Kara's hands. "You look exhausted."

"Been here since five," Kara admitted, rubbing her forehead. As Emma started cleaning, Kara let out a long breath, the words catching in her throat. "Em, I've been thinking, maybe it's time."

Emma paused mid-mop. "Time for?"

"To tell Charlotte about—you know. Everything."

Emma's eyes widened. "Whoa. You sure?"

Kara ran a hand through her hair. "Yesterday, seeing them together—and then her trying to get him to volunteer here. Em, she has no clue."

Emma winced. "Yeah, I noticed. And Ada didn't exactly help."

"Exactly." Kara sighed. "Besides, I can't keep this secret forever. She deserves to know."

Emma leaned on the mop. "Any idea how she might react?"

"No idea. To be honest, it scares me." She met Emma's eyes. "I'm just—" Kara shook her head. "I'm so grateful to have you, Em. Thanks for being my secret-keeper all this time."

Emma smiled. "Hey, that's what I'm here for." She nodded toward the doughnuts. "Now go on, take a break. We can talk more about it after you have a doughnut. I may have sampled one ... or two on the drive over." She shooed Kara away. "Go on, I'll finish up here."

"Okay, but only a quick one," Kara conceded, heading for the door. "I'll be right back."

⸎

Kara picked up a doughnut before stepping out the side door of the kennels. The crisp morning air filled her lungs as she leaned on the wall, taking a moment to appreciate the quiet. She examined the doughnut in her hand—a classic glazed with a drizzle of chocolate. As she bit into it, the sweet, pillowy softness melted on her tongue.

Kara closed her eyes, savoring the simple pleasure.

As she was about to take another bite, the rumble of an approaching engine caught her attention. Her eyes snapped open, and she saw a familiar blue Chevy pulling into the parking lot. She nearly choked on her doughnut before dropping what remained of it.

Heart racing, Kara quickly stepped back inside. As the door slammed behind her, barks erupted from the kennels.

Emma paused her mopping, yelling above the startled barks and yips, "Well, that was fast. How was the—"

"Em," Kara's voice shook. "Ethan's here. His truck just pulled up outside."

"What? Are you sure?" Emma set the mop aside.

Kara's gaze darted between Emma and the door. "Positive." Her pulse pounded in her ears, every second feeling like a countdown to disaster. "What do I do?"

"Say hey? Maybe he's signing up to volunteer."

Kara squeezed her eyes shut, her breath quickening.

She felt a hand on her shoulder. "Do you really not want to see him?" asked Emma.

"Yes. No. I don't know." Kara sighed. "I wasn't expecting him to come back so soon."

"Well, I can go out there and greet him. And you can stay back here. But you have to face the fact, Kara, you need help, whoever can help."

Emma's words triggered a flood of memories, transporting her back through time. The surrounding kennels began to fade, replaced by a different scene from her past ...

⁓ eee ⁓

The summer heat pressed against Kara, making her shirt stick to her back as she swept the sidewalk outside her dad's pharmacy. Behind her, the door stood propped open, letting the cool air-conditioned breeze occasionally brush against her skin.

As she swept, she caught sight of Ethan walking down the opposite side of the street, his shoulders hunched and hands shoved deep in his pockets. A group of guys passed by him, and Kara heard their snickers carried on the breeze.

"Hey, Bennett! Your old man sleep it off yet?" one of them shouted.

Kara saw Ethan hesitate, his step faltering for a second. He glanced back toward the guys, then quickly dropped his gaze to the ground and kept walking.

Her heart ached for him.

She set her broom against a shelf as she stepped inside the pharmacy. Her dad was behind the counter, sorting through a stack of papers.

"Dad, have you looked at Ethan's application yet?" Kara asked, trying to keep her voice casual.

Her dad sighed, pulling out a form from the stack. "Kara, we've been over this."

"But look at his qualifications." Kara insisted, pointing at the paper. "Honor roll, volunteer work at the hospital, and he even did that internship at the lab last summer. You'd hire anyone else with a resume like that in a heartbeat."

"I'm not hiring old drunk Bennett's son, Kara," her dad said, his voice firm. "That family's no good."

"But Ethan is nothing like his dad." Kara moved closer, grabbing her dad's arm. "He graduated with me. He's a really good guy, promise. Besides, we need the help. Whoever can help."

~ele~

"Kara ... Kara?" Emma's voice snapped Kara back to the present.

"Sorry, Em. I just—remembered something." Kara took a deep breath, squaring her shoulders. "You're right. We do need help, and I'm not gonna turn it down."

Emma smiled. "There's the Kara I know."

Kara then looked down at what she was wearing. "Great. Why did I think wearing Charlotte's high school gym shorts was a good fashion choice this morning? And this t-shirt. It has stains on it!" She groaned. "Never mind, nope, I can't let him see me like this."

"Nonsense. You didn't know he was going to be here," Emma said. "And you're working hard—it makes sense to wear comfortable clothes. Also, those shorts make your butt look great!"

Kara couldn't help but laugh as a layer of blush painted her cheeks. "Thanks, Em. You always know what to say."

Emma smirked, reaching out to pull her friend into a hug. "I do what I can."

Kara returned the hug, then stepped back. "Okay, I think I'm ready. I'm gonna talk to him." She paused, a new thought occurring to her. "Actually, Em, would you mind running into town to pick up a few supplies for the rescue?"

"Sure, I'll give y'all some alone time." Emma winked. "Anything specific you need?"

"You know, the usual—dog food, cat litter, and maybe some more cleaning supplies," Kara replied, reaching into her back pocket. "Use this." She pulled out the rescue's credit card and handed it to Emma, her fingers brushing over the raised numbers before letting go.

Emma took the card, tucking it into her pocket with a knowing smile. "You got it. Be back soon."

Kara watched as her friend slipped out, the door clicking shut behind her.

She glanced down at her clothes, grimacing at the stains on her shirt. She tried to smooth out the wrinkles and brush off some of the dog hair. A humorless chuckle escaped her lips.

What did it matter how she looked?

This was Ethan, after all.

Ethan, who had climbed through her window one night after a huge fight with her dad, just to bring her a pack of Oreos.

Ethan, who had covered for her at the pharmacy during that nightmarish inventory mix-up, shouldering the blame without hesitation when she'd accidentally flooded their stockroom with cough syrup instead of the much-needed allergy medication.

Ethan, who was Charlotte's father, and neither of them knew.

With another deep breath, she turned around slowly and began to walk toward the doors to the lobby.

12

Ethan

ETHAN GLANCED AROUND THE lobby of Second Chance Animal Rescue, his eyes drawn to pastel-colored bags of heart-shaped dog treats lining the reception desk. Something about their whimsical appearance made him smile.

"Ethan?" Kara's voice carried across the lobby.

He spun around and his heart stuttered as she stepped through the door.

"Oh, hey Kara." His voice cracked slightly. "I'm here to volunteer." He cleared his throat. "If you still need me, I mean my help, that is."

"Oh, um, sure. I mean, yes, that sounds, that sounds great!" She paused, seeming to gather herself. "We can definitely use the help."

A silence bloomed between them, stretching like taffy. Ethan's eyes darted back to the heart-shaped treats, as if they might whisper the perfect words to say next ...

"When we spoke yesterday, it, uh, it sounded like something fun to do while I'm in town. And I was curious to check the place out, so here I am."

Kara's gaze flickered to the corner before returning to him as though she were still deciding if letting him back into her world was a good idea. "Right, okay. How about we start with a quick tour?"

Ethan nodded. "Lead the way."

Kara gestured around them, her voice shifting to a more professional tone. "So, this is our lobby. Normally, we'd have someone at the desk handling questions, arranging animal visits, that sort of thing. Anyway, the kennels are through here."

As Kara turned back toward the doors that led to the kennels, Ethan rushed over and grabbed one of the handles, holding the door open for her, which started up the cacophony of barks.

She smiled.

He grinned—like a fool.

Swallowing hard, he stepped inside after her and was struck by how clean the place was. The floors gleamed, and there wasn't a trace of the typical animal rescue smell he'd been bracing himself for.

Kara raised her voice over the barking. "Welcome to the kennels! Some dogs are still in the yard—I was cleaning when you arrived. Mind if we pause the tour to bring them in?"

"No problem," Ethan said, rolling up his sleeves.

Kara's face brightened. "Let me get the leashes."

Ethan followed Kara down the aisles and over to a door in the corner where pegs were adorned with an array of different-colored leashes ranging in every size.

Kara reached for a bundle of them. "Think you can handle leashing them up? Then we can walk them back."

"Sure thing," Ethan said with a nod. "After you."

Bright sunlight streamed through the doorway as Ethan stepped outside. The yard was alive with activity thanks to a motley crew of canines, from a towering Great Dane to a tiny Chihuahua, and everything in between. Some chased each other in playful circles, while others were content to roll in the grass, tongues lolling out in canine bliss.

Ethan noted how the grass, well-maintained and lush, still sparkled with traces of morning dew. A majestic oak tree stood at the far end, providing a patch of shade. Then he saw the bounty of canine entertainment: tennis balls, brightly colored frisbees, and an array of squeaky toys strewn about like offerings for the ruling pups of this domain.

"This must be what Dog Heaven looks like."

Kara's melodious laughter tickled his ears.

Ethan scanned the scene, counting the dogs. *One, two, three ... seven, eight ...* He lost track somewhere in the mid-teens, and decided to just take a tangle of leashes from Kara's outstretched hand. The cool metal clips created a soft chime as they collided.

"There are so many of them." Ethan's eyes widened. "Must take a small army to manage everything."

The corners of Kara's mouth lifted in a smile that was equal parts pride and exhaustion. "It's actually just me most days," she said with a shrug. "Hasn't always been like this, but you know how things change."

Ethan snapped his head around. "Wait, what? How do you even—I mean, that's amazing."

Kara was already moving toward a nearby dog. "You figure it out as you go. Come on, let's get these pups inside."

They set about rounding up the dogs, their conversation minimal. Kara's tone remained professional as she offered tidbits of information about the rescue, making Ethan feel oddly like a stranger. But instead of dwelling on it, he focused on the task at hand.

Corralling the excited pups was like herding caffeinated butterflies, but eventually, they guided almost every dog back to their kennel. As they worked, Ethan noticed the path her feet had etched into the yard's perimeter, the ballet-like grace of her efficient movements, and the way each dog's ears perked up at her familiar footsteps. Finally, they came to the last dog, a miniature schnauzer, who seemed intent on sleeping in the shade under the large oak.

Kara held out a leash. "That's Benny. Why don't you take him?"

Ethan, taking the leash, lowered himself to eye level with the miniature schnauzer. "Hey there, Benny," He stroked the gray fur on top of his head. "You enjoying some time in the shade?" Ethan smiled. "How old's this guy?"

"Twelve, we think. He came in as a stray about six years ago."

"Six years? And no one's adopted him yet?"

Kara kneeled beside Ethan. "He's had a few foster homes," she explained, her voice soft. "But it never quite worked out. One family moved, another was allergic, and the last—well, senior dog care isn't cheap."

Ethan scratched behind Benny's ears. "Poor guy. Any interest lately?"

Kara shook her head. "Not yet. But his forever home is out there somewhere. He's such a sweetheart."

Ethan clipped the leash to Benny's collar. "What do you say, Benny? Ready?"

As they walked back inside, Kara pointed out various storage areas, explaining, "Here's where we keep our extra bedding ... food ... and other supplies."

Ethan nodded, taking it all in. "You only rescue dogs?"

"No, we usually have cats too, but it's been quiet on that front lately."

They paused by a window, sunlight streaming in and illuminating Kara's face. Her small smile faded, replaced by a quiet intensity. "You know, when we first started, we only rescued cats and dogs. Didn't make much sense though when really all animals feel pain and joy, like any pet."

Ethan listened intently, captivated by the passion in her voice.

Kara continued. "Every animal wants to live. It's a shame that they're treated differently because they weren't born a cat or dog. They all deserve compassion and care. That's what this place is about, a home for all animals who need a second chance." Kara's face lit up. "You wouldn't believe some animals we've rescued. Goats, chickens, and, believe it or not, a pretentious frog who thought he was a prince."

Ethan raised an eyebrow. "No kidding? Where'd you put them all?"

"We made do here for a while, but eventually found them homes at better-equipped rescues. Oh, and get this—we once rescued a pig that jumped off a truck headed for, well, you know."

Ethan shook his head. "Kara, that's—wow." He met her eyes. "What you're doing here—it's incredible, really."

Kara's cheeks flushed. "Thanks. It's tough sometimes, but—" She glanced around at the animals. "Each one matters, you know?"

"They do, and they're lucky to have you." Ethan smiled, then clapped his hands together. "So, what's next on the to-do list?"

Kara bit her lip. "Actually, there is something. I've got this camera I've been meaning to install in the yard. Keep an eye on the dogs, you know? Just haven't found the time." She jerked her thumb toward a door. "I'll grab it from the office. Mind getting the ladder and toolbox from the supply closet?"

"On it," Ethan said, already moving. As he opened the door to the walk-in closet, he blinked at the clutter inside. A mishmash of items crowded the shelves—giant bottles of pet shampoo stood beside squeaky toys, while a leaning tower of creased animal care guides looked ready to collapse.

As his eyes scanned inside, finding the ladder and toolbox, something else caught his attention. A photo album, its spine labeled *Second Chance Animal Rescue*, sat on top of a pile of blankets.

He carefully pulled it out and opened the album. Page after page showed Kara over the years, her smile constant even as the scenery and animals around her changed.

As he neared the back of the album, something slipped

from between the pages. He reached out and caught it before it hit the floor. Ethan's chest tightened.

It was a Polaroid. Kara's eyes were closed, caught mid-blink, while he sported a wide, carefree smile from twenty-two years ago.

She kept it?

"Ethan?" Kara called out. "You okay in there?"

Ethan fumbled with the album, tucking the Polaroid back into its place and returning the album to its spot on the pile. He grabbed the ladder, his heart still pounding.

"Yeah, got 'em!" he called back. He took a steadying breath before stepping out of the closet. "Got lost in there for a second," he added with a chuckle.

"Yeah, that closet has been lurking on my to-do list since, well—" Kara's face scrunched into a rueful grimace. "Probably since we opened," she admitted with a self-deprecating chuckle. "Never enough hours in the day."

Ethan followed Kara outside and waited while she decided on the best spot for the camera.

Kara squinted up at the corner of the building. "What about up there? Think that'd work?"

Ethan tilted his head. "Hard to tell from down here. Can we check the feed before we mount it?"

She dug into her pocket for her phone. "Oh, right. There's an app." She waved the phone. "Mind holding it up there while I check?"

Ethan nodded, setting up the ladder. "No problem. I'll head up. Pass it to me?"

Kara gripped the base, steadying it. "Okay, but watch your step. This ladder's about as old as the barn itself."

"Well, that's comforting."

Kara shrugged, a sheepish grin on her face. "It was here when we renovated the barn. Never got a new one."

Ethan smirked. "So, you're perfectly fine with me scaling this relic that probably witnessed the stock market crash of '29?"

Kara laughed, swatting his arm. "Oh, stop it! It's not that old. Just well-loved."

Ethan started up the ladder. "If I fall, at least it's a short trip."

When Kara handed the camera and its mount to him, his hand tingled from the brief contact with hers. The simple touch sent a jolt through him, stirring a memory. The warm sunlight dimmed, giving way to the glow of fluorescent lights ...

The soft beep of the pharmacy's cash register hummed in the background as Kara stood beside him, her chestnut hair pulled back in a ponytail, a name tag pinned to her shirt.

"So, after you scan the items," Kara said, leaning in close enough that Ethan could catch a whiff of her light, jasmine perfume, "you just press this button here." Her voice had a playful lilt to it, as if she was sharing a secret.

As she reached out to demonstrate, her hand brushed against his. The touch lingered a fraction longer than necessary. He looked up, meeting Kara's eyes. For a moment, he saw a flicker of something in her gaze—surprise? Interest?

She glanced away, a faint blush coloring her cheeks.

"And, um, that's all you do," she said, tucking a stray strand behind her ear.

"Seems simple enough. But maybe you should show me one more time?" He flashed her a grin. "Just to make sure I've got it down."

Kara laughed, bumping her shoulder against his. "Really?"

"Well, you know what they say. Practice makes perfect."

After showing him one more time, Kara raised an eyebrow. "Alright, hotshot. Let's see what you've learned." She grabbed a random item from the counter. "Ring me up."

As Ethan fiddled with the scanner, hyper-aware of Kara's proximity, he couldn't help but think that learning the cash register was suddenly the most exciting thing in the world.

***

The memory faded like a passing breeze, leaving him standing on the ladder again, holding the camera. He blinked, refocusing as he positioned it.

"How's it look?" Ethan adjusted his grip. "We good?"

"Hang on ... stupid app ... Ah! There we go." She squinted at the screen. "Okay, maybe nudge it right a bit? And tilt it ... yeah, like that."

Ethan shifted the camera. "Better?"

"That's it! Perfect."

Ethan glanced down. "Pass me the drill? And grab a couple screws, would you?"

Kara rummaged in the toolbox, grabbing the drill and a handful of screws. She looked up, their gazes caught for a moment. "These okay?"

Ethan took the drill, eyeing the screws. "Yeah, that'll do. Can you hand them to me one by one?"

As Ethan worked on mounting the camera, Kara stood close, ready with each screw. Every time she passed one to him, there was a moment—a shared look, a subtle smile, a barely-there touch of fingers, like the start of something they weren't quite ready to admit.

Ethan made quick work of mounting the camera on the side of the building, though part of him wished the task would last longer.

After he was done, he descended the ladder. "All set," he said, turning to face her.

They stood there for a moment, neither moving away,

"I should, uh—" Ethan gestured at the ladder. "Probably put this back."

"Oh! Right, yeah." Kara tucked a loose strand of hair behind her ear. "I've got the toolbox."

Once inside, they put away the ladder and toolbox, then Kara pulled out her phone and showed Ethan the camera app. "This is perfect. I can finally keep tabs on the yard without running out every five minutes."

"Happy to help." Ethan smiled, shoving his hands in his pockets as he glanced toward the kennels. "Anything else on your list?"

Kara sighed. "Nothing for now. The animals are good until tonight. I'll probably be answering emails and catching up on planning until then."

Ethan took a step back. "Guess I should let you get to it then." He paused. "This was—nice. You need help tomorrow?"

"Oh, I mean." Kara's eyes flitted about the room. "If you're free, that is. You probably have plans."

"I could swing by. Same time?"

"Yeah. Yeah, that'd be great."

"Great! It's a date—not a *date* date, you know ..." It was his turn to blush. "Tomorrow then."

13

Kara

STEPPING OUT INTO THE lobby, Kara watched through the large plate-glass window. A wave of melancholy washed over her as Ethan's truck disappeared down the main road. Releasing a deep breath, she turned from the window and walked back toward the reception desk, rounding the corner as the door swung open from the opposite end. She nearly collided with Emma, her breath catching as she spotted the takeout bags swinging from her friend's arms.

"Thought you might be hungry, so I grabbed something from Phil's after grabbing the supplies," Emma said.

Kara's mouth began to water as the aroma from the bags hit her nostrils. "Is that the new Beyond Cheesesteak?"

Emma reached into one of the bags, pulling out a slightly steaming styrofoam box and handing it to Kara with a flourish.

"With extra banana peppers?"

Emma put her hand on her hip. "Now, what kind of friend

would I be if I didn't get extra banana peppers on your sub?"

"Ah, you're the best."

"Hey, why don't we eat outside? It's gorgeous today," Emma said, walking toward the side door. "Come on. We'll sit at the table."

Kara followed Emma to the side yard, where a small picnic table waited. Spreading out everything on the table, they went to sit down. But as Kara was about to take her seat, she hesitated, glancing back towards the building. "Don't we need to unload your car with all the supplies—"

"It can wait," Emma said, patting the bench next to her. "The rescue ain't gonna fall apart if you take a ten-minute break. Sit. Eat. Relax."

Realizing how tense she'd been, Kara made a conscious effort to relax her shoulders, before releasing a quiet sigh as she settled across from Emma. "Yeah, you're right. I guess I'm always on edge about this place." She flipped open the box, revealing the steaming Beyond Cheesesteak sub nestled in its paper wrapper. The aroma of sautéed peppers and onions wafted up, making her stomach growl.

"This smells incredible," Kara gushed, picking up the sub. "Think it'll live up to the hype?"

"Only one way to find out." Emma held up her own sub in a mock toast. "Cheers to trying new things and awesome friends."

They each took a big bite, their eyes widening as they savored the flavors. For a few blissful moments, the only sounds were those of contented chewing, the gentle whisper of leaves from the lone oak tree swaying nearby in the breeze, and the cheerful chatter of birds flitting among its branches.

"This is so good!" Emma said between bites, but when Kara didn't respond right away, she raised an eyebrow. "So, how did it go with Ethan? Anything happen?"

Kara reached for a napkin. "Nothing really."

Emma sighed. "Nothing really?"

Kara nodded. "Yeah, nothing."

"Come on, spill." Emma leaned in. "Was it as awkward as you were thinking?

Kara put her sub down and leaned onto the table. "No, not really. It was okay. He helped bring in the dogs and set up that security camera."

"You've been wanting to put that up forever now!"

"I know. He helped me out a ton today." Kara looked down. "It was nice of him."

"So strictly business? Nothing about the past got brought up?"

An unexpected tingle traveled up her arm as she recalled the fleeting moment their fingers brushed. "I don't think there's anything there." Her eyes flickered down. "He's just killing time while he's around. That's it."

"That redness in your cheeks would say otherwise," Emma said.

Kara took a deep breath, shaking her head, avoiding eye contact.

"You don't have to be embarrassed, you know. I mean, this guy meant a lot to you once upon a time. Y'all started hanging out right after high school graduation, right?"

"Yeah, that summer when we were working together at the pharmacy."

Emma took a bite of her sub. "Right, I remember that."

"It feels like a lifetime ago." Kara paused, her thumb idly tracing the edge of the table. "He kissed me one night when we were closing the pharmacy, and I guess that's when everything started." A smile graced her lips. "Mom knew about us. She loved him." Then her happiness flatlined. "Dad didn't know until after the accident."

The sound of chewing stopped and Kara looked at her friend, whose dark brown eyes were filled with warmth and sympathy.

"You don't have to keep going." Emma reached out to grab Kara's hand. "I didn't mean to bring all that up, was just trying to remember what you had told me before is all."

Kara let out a sigh. "No, it's—it's fine. It doesn't sting like it used to. Thinking about Ethan and me. But the way he just up and left without a word after that night on the beach." She shook her head. "And right when I was dealing with losing Mom." Her sub sat on the wax paper it came packaged in, looking anything but appetizing now. "What was I thinking? I waited for a call, a letter—anything."

"Did you consider asking him about it today? Why he ghosted you like that?"

"I mean, yeah, it crossed my mind. But how do you even bring that up? Besides, I'm not sure I want to open that can of worms. He's coming back tomorrow to finish up, and—"

"Tomorrow? That doesn't sound like someone who's just 'killing time.'"

"Heh, I'm not getting my hopes up or anything. He'll be gone soon. Better if we keep things strictly professional."

Emma studied Kara's face. "There's something else bothering you, isn't there?"

Kara met Emma's gaze. "How are you so good at that?"

"It's the power of being a best friend."

"Right, well, I can't stop thinking about telling him about Charlotte—and Charlotte about him. I know I need to, but once again, where do I even start? How do I drop that bomb on either of them?"

"That's—" Emma nodded, her tone softening. "Yeah, that's huge."

"I'm terrified, Em." Kara's voice dropped to barely a whisper. "What if Charlotte hates me for keeping the truth from her? What if Ethan ..." She trailed off, her stomach tightening at the thought of seeing the hurt—or worse, the anger—in Ethan's eyes when he found out.

Emma reached across the table and squeezed Kara's hand. "Hey, you've faced tough situations before. Remember when you had to testify against that puppy mill last year?"

Kara nodded, a faint smile playing on her lips. "It wasn't easy."

"And you crushed it, Kara. Granted, this is a whole different ball game, I know, but you've got this too."

A gust of wind swept through, catching the edges of Kara's styrofoam box. It wobbled, lifting off the table. She quickly placed her hand on top, the sudden motion making her heart skip for a second.

"But when's the right time? How do I even begin?

"There's never going to be a perfect moment for something like this. But Ethan being here? That might be the opening you need. Remember, you don't have to solve everything in one go."

Kara exhaled, feeling some of the tension leave her shoulders. Her gaze drifted back to the rescue, reminding her of all she had built here—and all she had yet to confront. "You're right, as usual. I just need to take that first step."

"And you will, Kara." Emma reached over and grabbed her hand, giving it a squeeze. "And don't worry about when or how. When the time's right, you'll know."

"Yeah," said Kara, not too convinced, eyes dragging back down to her sandwich—but still, she didn't touch it.

Emma squeezed her hand. "Kara, look at me."

Kara sighed but did as her friend requested.

"You're not alone in this either. I'll be right here when you need me. Okay?"

14

Ethan

THE SCENTS OF PRODUCE and freshly baked bread greeted him as Ethan pushed through the glass door and mentally ticked off items: something to make for a few meals and a few more cans of dog food for Hero. He grabbed a cart and started down the first aisle. Plucking a crisp head of lettuce and a bag of bright orange carrots from the display, his mind wandered back to the animal rescue and the eventful day he'd spent there.

Despite her attempts to hide it, he couldn't help but notice how much she was struggling. After all, the rescue was chronically understaffed by her own admission. He felt a twinge of concern for Kara and the animals in her care.

What can I do to help?

At the rescue he'd worked at in Virginia, they had thrown regular adoption events and fundraisers that had always gone over well. Second Chance had hosted a big event just yesterday, yet the kennels were still full, so it seemed like they needed more than just occasional events to keep up with the influx of animals. Perhaps a more consistent volunteer base could be the start of turning things around? Lost in thought, Ethan absently navigated the grocery aisles ...

Wheeling his cart around the corner, a wry smile tugged at his lips as he realized the familiar arrangement of shelves and products had remained unchanged since he had last visited over twenty years ago. He passed by the rows of condiments and jars of pickles. Stopping at the pasta sauce, he grabbed a jar and picked up a box of rigatoni, then headed to the next aisle. Then he scanned the shelves for dog food and handpicked several cans, stacking them in his arms.

While juggling the cans and steering his cart, Ethan rounded the corner and froze, nearly dropping the dog food. His breath caught in his throat as his eyes locked onto an all-too-familiar face. A cold sweat prickled Ethan's skin as his heart hammered against his ribs.

That's when Whitaker Walker's eyes narrowed in recognition.

With trembling hands, Ethan spun his cart around and beelined for the nearest checkout, where he haphazardly scooped items from his cart and dumped them onto the conveyor belt. He fumbled for a few bills to pay the cashier. "Keep the change."

"Need a hand with those bags, sir?" the cashier asked.

Ethan shook his head and grabbed the bags, hurrying out of the store as quickly as he could without running, not daring to look back to see if Whitaker was watching him.

He tossed the bagged groceries onto the passenger seat, struggled to find his keys before cranking the engine to life, and reversed out of the spot with a screech from the tires.

At a red light, Ethan briefly closed his eyes, inhaling deeply, remembering the calming techniques Dr. Hartman had taught him.

"Four ... seven ... eight ..." Ethan mumbled under his breath.

Even as he counted, his heart drummed in his chest, refusing to settle. When the light turned green, he forced his foot back on the gas, determined to focus on his breathing. He inhaled deeply through his nose for a count of four ... held it for seven ... then exhaled slowly through his mouth for eight, repeating this pattern at every stop.

By the time he made the last turn into the driveway of his dad's house, Ethan's breathing had steadied, though his hands still gave way to a slight tremble.

He put the truck in park, sat for a moment, and continued the exercise.

"In, two, three, four ..." he whispered, inhaling. He held the breath, counting silently to seven. Then, "Out, two, three, four, five, six, seven, eight," as he exhaled slowly.

Several deep breaths later, the tremors in Ethan's hands had eased enough for him to collect his groceries, paper bags crinkling as he reached the front door, unlocking it.

Ethan stumbled inside, greeted by Hero sprawled on the living room rug. Hero sprang up and walked over to him, following him to the kitchen.

On the counter, Ethan grabbed his bottle of meds, opened it, and took out a pill. Then he filled a glass at the sink and swallowed. Glancing down at the bottle, he realized he was down to his last couple of pills.

Ethan frowned, recalling his last conversation with Dr. Hartman.

When did she say the refill would be ready?

Ethan placed the bottle back on the counter, positioning it prominently so he wouldn't forget. He even set a reminder on his phone, just in case. For now, though, he needed to put away the groceries.

Leaning against the counter, Ethan smiled as Hero padded over, tail wagging. "Hey, buddy," Ethan said, reaching out to scratch behind Hero's ears. "How'd you do while I was gone? Kept the house safe for me?"

Hero barked, pressing his head into Ethan's hand.

Ethan chuckled. "I'll take that as a yes. Now, how about we get these groceries put away, and maybe we can go for a walk?"

At the word 'walk,' Hero's ears perked, and he barked again.

"All right, all right," Ethan grinned. "Let's take care of business first."

When Ethan began unpacking the grocery bags, Hero trotted after him, nose twitching with interest at the various scents. Then as Ethan reached for a can of dog food, his phone buzzed. He glanced at the screen.

"Mr. Clark," he muttered, recognizing the attorney's number.

With a deep breath, he answered the call. "Hey, Mr. Clark."

"Ethan, good to catch you. I'm calling to check on your

progress."

"The deed, right. Look, I've been—" Ethan sighed, running a hand through his hair. "It's been a lot. I sorted through some mail, but that's about it. This weekend was—complicated. I just got back actually."

Ethan watched as Hero trotted to the doggy door and slipped outside.

"This deed is crucial. Without it, the house can't be sold. And if I recall correctly, you were quite insistent on a quick sale. Yes?"

Ethan blinked, snapping back to the call. "I get it, Mr. Clark, I do. Trust me, I want out of here as soon as possible. I'll find the deed, even if I have to tear this place apart today."

⁓ℓℓ⁓

It had been seven hours, and still, the deed was nowhere to be found, despite Ethan's best efforts in turning the small house upside down. At first, he was methodical; then, with increasing desperation as the deed continued to elude him, reckless.

Hero followed closely behind, sniffing curiously at the now-scattered items.

He'd started in the living room, upending the old couch cushions and checking behind the familiar framed photos on the walls. The kitchen had been next—every cabinet emptied, even the freezer searched on the off chance his dad had stashed it there one drunken night.

The bathroom yielded nothing but the same old medicine cabinet contents and the sink that had always dripped. In his bedroom, Ethan yanked the faded blue comforter from the bed, rifled through every pocket of the clothes still hanging in the pine wardrobe, and crawled under the creaky twin bed he'd outgrown years ago, emerging with cobwebs in his hair that he combed out with his fingers. He sifted through stacks of old newspapers and books that had accumulated over decades, and even searched inside the TV he and his dad used to watch ballgames, half-convinced his dad could've hollowed it out as a secret hiding spot.

Hero grabbed at the loose papers, thinking Ethan was playing a game. Ethan gently shooed him away. "Not now, boy."

Standing in the hallway, amid the chaos of his search, Ethan crossed his arms and kicked an empty cardboard box aside. The house was a mess, every surface covered in displaced items. Clutter filled the corners, a lifetime's accumulation of possessions strewn about—old tools from his dad's workdays, clothes Ethan had long outgrown, and knick-knacks collected over years of tight budgets and simple living.

On the way to the kitchen, Ethan froze. There was one place he hadn't checked.

Dad's closet.

With fresh resolve, he strode to the master bedroom. The closet door groaned on its hinges as he pulled it open, revealing a jumble of clothes and boxes. As he searched, his hand brushed against something he knew well, like an old song—his dad's Marine dress blues. The crisp fabric and polished buttons shone even in the dim light. He reached out, running his fingers along the sleeve of the dress coat.

A memory flashed—six-year-old Ethan, standing before the mirror, drowning in his dad's uniform coat. The sleeves hanging well past his hands, the hem nearly touching the floor, his dad's warm laughter filling the room.

"You'll grow into it someday, kiddo," his dad had said, ruffling Ethan's hair.

Ethan blinked against the sudden sting in his eyes and turned toward a shoebox tucked in the closet's corner. Inside, he found postcards and small mementos from the patchwork of places they'd called home over the years. Hero settled beside him, resting his head on Ethan's knee as he sifted through fragments of their nomadic past.

A faded postcard of a magnolia blossom brought back memories of the sweltering Mississippi heat. Ethan remembered the tiny apartment they'd shared, his dad working long hours at a shipyard while Ethan adapted to yet another new school.

Next, he picked up a small carved wooden bison. North Dakota—where winter seemed to last forever, and the wind never stopped howling. His dad had found work on an oil rig, and often came home exhausted but somehow always made time to help Ethan with his homework.

Then a keychain shaped like the Liberty Bell transported Ethan to their longest stretch in one place—Pennsylvania. His dad had initially thrived on the city's energy, securing a steady job in Philadelphia. But as years passed, the pressures of city life took their toll. The overtime hours grew longer, and Ethan watched his dad's drinking evolve from a few beers after work to a nightly ritual, with a growing collection of bottles in the recycling bin, carefully hidden under newspapers.

Ethan learned to recognize the slight slur in his dad's speech, the stumbling gait as he came home later and later. The smell of whiskey became a constant presence, clinging to his old man's clothes and breath. Memories of those years were mixed with bright spots—trips to Independence Hall, Phillies games—and darker moments of arguments and broken promises.

Finally, his fingers closed around a small ceramic lighthouse, a souvenir from their first day in Hadley Cove. Ethan remembered the day clearly—His dad, sober and grinning, had picked it up at a quaint shop on the boardwalk.

"This is our second chance, son," he'd said, his eyes clear for the first time in years. "We're going to make a real home here."

His dad had secured a job at a local factory, thanks to an old Marine buddy. For a while, it seemed like things were looking up. The small town's peaceful atmosphere appeared to have a positive effect, and Ethan dared to hope that this time things would be different.

But as weeks turned into months, familiar patterns emerged. It started with "just one beer" after a long shift, then a few more. Soon, Ethan was finding hidden bottles around the house again. The ceramic lighthouse, once proudly displayed on the mantel, had been knocked over during one of his dad's stumbling late-night returns. Now, it sat in this closet as a chipped reminder of what could have been but never was.

Ethan sighed, gently setting down the lighthouse. Near

it, he pushed aside a stack of old flannel shirts before his hand struck something solid. He cleared away more debris, revealing a small safe tucked into the corner. His heart raced.

Could this be it?

Pulling the safe out, his hands shook slightly as he examined it. It was an old model, probably as old as he was, with a keyhole on the front. He ran his fingers over the cool metal, searching for any hidden compartments where his dad may have stashed the key, but found nothing.

Ethan glanced around the closet, hoping to spot a key hanging on a nail or tucked into a pocket, but came up empty. He even checked the pockets of the Marine dress blues, thinking his dad might have hidden it there, but no luck.

Glancing at his phone and registering the late hour, he carefully placed the safe on his dad's old dresser with a sigh.

I'll get a locksmith tomorrow.

15

Kara

Monday

As Kara waited for Ethan's arrival, she threw herself into the morning chores. She fed the dogs, filled their water bowls, let them out into the yard for their bathroom breaks, and performed basic health checks on each animal ... By the time she finished, nearly three hours had passed.

Where could he be?

Kara paced the worn linoleum, her eyes flicking to the clock every few seconds. The makeup she'd applied earlier—something she rarely bothered with—now felt like a mistake. Doubts crept in, echoing the disappointments of the past.

Did I say something wrong yesterday? Maybe he's changed his mind about coming, just like he changed his mind about calling.

She shook her head, pushing the thoughts away.

Why do I even care what he thinks?

Kara began shuffling through papers on the reception desk when the lobby door swung open and Ethan walked in.

"Kara, I'm so sorry I'm late. I—"

"You could've called," Kara cut in.

A heavy silence fell between them. Kara's cheeks flushed as she realized how sharp her words had sounded.

Kara sighed. "Look, I'm sorry. That came out wrong. I really do appreciate you being here."

Ethan shifted on his feet, running a hand through his hair. "No, you're right. I should've called. This morning's been a disaster."

His eyes flicked to hers. He let out a sigh and licked his lips before continuing. "Had to call a locksmith to the house. They kept saying 'soon,' you know? But after waiting forever, turns out they can't make it till later, whenever that is."

Another quiet stretch settled between them as Kara listened, half-wondering what his excuse was for twenty-two years ago, half-tempted to add this to the growing tally of letdowns in her mind. Yet she couldn't take her eyes off him, watching as he glanced around the lobby like some shamed puppy.

It was her turn to sigh.

He offered an apologetic smile. "So, uh, where do you want me to start?"

"Mom!"

Kara and Ethan both turned to face the side door. "Charlotte?"

Kara watched her daughter's eyes grow wide as she

stepped into the lobby at the unexpected presence of—
"Ethan!"

For a moment, the three of them stood in silence—Kara caught between her daughter and her past, Ethan looking slightly out of place, and Charlotte's eyes ping-ponging between the two.

Kara blinked, swallowing hard. "Charlotte, weren't you supposed to be with friends today?"

"Yeah, plans fell through. Thought I'd make myself useful here instead." Turning to the familiar face, she extended a polite greeting. "Good morning, Ethan. Decided to volunteer after all?"

Ethan nodded. "That's right. Nice to see you again, Charlotte."

"Likewise," Charlotte replied, then clapped her hands together. "All right, Mom, what's on the agenda?"

Kara put her hands on her hips. "Let's start with the kennels."

Ethan held open the double doors, letting Charlotte and Kara walk through first. Excited barks and whines filled the air, with eager paws scratching at kennel gates as they walked down the aisle.

Kara scanned the room. "Okay, here's what we'll do. We're gonna work in shifts, grouping the dogs strategically." She turned to Charlotte. "You'll start by taking out our social butterflies—Freckles, Oliver, Penny, Juniper, and Pepper—into the yard."

Charlotte gave a mock salute. "Aye aye, captain."

"Ethan," Kara continued, "while Charlotte has that group out, you'll change the bedding in their empty cages. I'll handle the mopping. Then we'll rotate through the more skittish dogs, the seniors, and finally the puppies. This way, we can clean more efficiently and cater to each group's needs."

Ethan nodded. "Smart setup, Kara. I'll get right on it."

As they set to work, Kara marveled at the seamless rhythm that they quickly established, moving around each other with an almost choreographed efficiency. Tasks that usually consumed her entire day seemed to fly by with their combined effort. How long had it been since she had help with daily chores? She'd almost forgotten what it felt like.

With the afternoon carrying on, Kara couldn't help but watch Charlotte and Ethan interact. The similarities between them were striking—not only their physical features, but their mannerisms, and the way they approached tasks. When it came time to take out the senior dogs, Kara watched as Ethan gently helped Charlotte with Benny, taking special care in securing the leash and guiding the old dog to the yard. Then when it came time for the puppies the two must have spent thirty minutes snuggling and playing with the little fuzz balls. The ease with which they clicked—it was almost too much.

He doesn't even know she's his.

The thought stabbed at her heart, but now wasn't the time.

Soon. I'll tell him soon. Both of them.

Just then, Charlotte's melodious laughter rang out, light and carefree, pulling Kara from her thoughts. It was in response to one of Ethan's playful remarks, and the sound tugged at Kara's heart. Blinking rapidly to clear her eyes, she drew in a deep breath to steady herself. With a quiet exhale, she turned back to the task at hand, pulling out the bedding from the next cage.

The work continued steadily, the familiar scent of disinfectant and lemon cleaner filling the air and mingling with the occasional bark or whine. The cool linoleum floor squeaked beneath her feet as she moved from cage to cage. When she neared the end of the cleaning routine, Kara heard the back door open and turned.

Ethan had stepped inside, wiping his hands on his jeans, leaving faint streaks behind. "Last bunch is all set in the shade," he reported, reaching for a fresh bag of bedding. "How's it going on this end?"

Kara gestured to the nearly finished row. "Getting there. Got these last few left."

As Ethan joined her in tackling the remaining row of kennels, Kara decided to take a chance on some casual conversation. "So, where are you living now?"

"Virginia," he answered. "Been there for a while, after I left the army." Ethan took over pulling the bedding from the cages.

Kara noticed a faint scar on Ethan's forearm. Without thinking, she reached out, her fingers hovering above his skin. "Is that from—?"

"Yeah, from my time in the service." Ethan glanced down, tracing an invisible line around the wound. "It's all healed up now, though."

Kara nodded, withdrawing her hand. "I saw about the Silver Star in the paper."

Ethan shrugged. "Just did what needed to be done," he

murmured. "What about you? Have you been in Hadley Cove this whole time?"

Kara let out a soft, wistful laugh. "You mean for the past two decades? Yeah, I've been here. Never saw a reason to leave, you know? And then with the rescue. Well, it kept me here." She paused. "Plus, with Charlotte, I figured a place like this would be good for her. Stable, you know?"

"Well, it seems like you raised her right. She's a good kid."

Kara chewed on her bottom lip. "She is—she's wonderful."

The words hung in the air, and Kara felt the weight of her unspoken truth pressing down on her. Her heart raced as she imagined the possible outcomes.

What if he storms out, and I never see him again?

Or what if… What if he wants to be part of our lives?

What if he says he wants to, but never calls?

Kara took a deep breath, the conflicting scenarios swirling in her mind.

I have to tell him. Both of them. Soon. But how?

"Kara?"

Stumbling out of her thoughts, Kara looked up. "Yeah? Sorry, I was just—yeah, what's up?"

Ethan's voice pulled her back. "Were you gonna mop these kennels?" he asked, reaching for the mop. "Because if not, I can do it."

"Of course! Sorry." She looked up at him and smiled. "I can do it—I don't mind."

"Sure." Ethan's fingers lingered on the mop handle before he let go, and Kara took a second to gather herself, pushing away the small knot of nerves in her stomach.

Relax, it's just Ethan. Like old times ... Sort of.

Ethan smirked. "You know, this brings back memories."

"Oh?"

"Yeah, like closing up shop at the pharmacy, remember?"

Kara laughed. "You mean when you always made me mop the floor? I don't think I remember you doing it even once!"

"That was wrong of me," he admitted. Then, with a playful glint in his eye, he added, "but to be fair, I did have to take the trash out every night. You wouldn't even touch the bins."

Kara rolled her eyes. "Well, trash was clearly a man's job, wasn't it?"

"And I guess mopping was a woman's job." Ethan pulled the mop out of her hands. "Thankfully I don't share that same narrow-minded view of my yesteryears."

Kara snorted. "Yesteryears? Who are you, my grandpa?"

Ethan leaned dramatically on the mop, hunching over. "Get off my lawn, you whippersnapper!"

Laughter filled the space as Charlotte walked back inside. "What'd I miss?"

Kara waved her hand dismissively, still grinning. "Just old people talk, honey. How are the dogs doing?"

"Pretty good. The senior pups are all chilling in the shade. Tried to start a game of fetch, but no takers." She glanced around the kennels. "You guys making progress in here?"

"Almost done." Kara glanced over at Ethan, smiling. "Ethan is gonna mop the rest of the cages, and we've got all the bedding changed. This has gotta be some kind of record. Made a world of difference with y'all here, that's for sure."

Charlotte flashed a grin and tossed her hair with exaggerated flair. "Oh Mom, what can I say? I'm simply irreplaceable."

Ethan's lips quirked into a smile. "Anytime. Actually enjoyed myself."

Once they had everything cleaned and the dogs were back in their kennels, Charlotte, Ethan, and Kara walked back out into the lobby. Kara stole glances at Ethan, noting how easily he had fit into their routine. The day had flown by, and she realized she wasn't ready for it to end.

Ethan seemed to sense her gaze and turned, catching her eye. For a moment, they stood there, the air between them charged with unspoken words and shared memories. Kara opened her mouth, unsure of what she was about to say, when Charlotte's voice cut through the moment.

"So, any plans for later?" Charlotte said, turning to Ethan.

"Got some work to do at Dad's place. Then I was thinking about hitting up Phil's for dinner." He glanced between Kara and Charlotte. "What about you two? Any plans?"

Kara looked over at Charlotte. "Well, we were—"

Charlotte's eyes lit up. "Oh, Mom is completely free tonight!" She nudged Kara with her elbow. "You should totally go with him, Mom."

"Charlotte, I—"

"I would go too, but I have a date with Netflix and a pack of Oreos," Charlotte continued, winking at Ethan.

Ethan chuckled. "Hard to compete with that."

Charlotte snapped her fingers. "Oh! That reminds me. I heard what Ada said at the adoption event." She looked between Kara and Ethan, her eyebrows raised. "Were you two really a thing back in the day?"

Kara's heart dropped, and she hesitated. "Uh, we—"

Ethan jumped in, "We were friends. Worked at the pharmacy together one summer."

Kara's smile wavered for a moment, the word 'friends' echoing in her mind.

Is that really all it was?

She swallowed the lump forming in her throat. Maybe it was better this way—keeping things simple. But the secret she was keeping felt like a tightening knot in her chest, winding more with each moment.

"Ahh, I see," Charlotte nodded. "Well, I guess your *friend* date should be fun." She emphasized 'friend' with exaggerated air quotes.

"Charlotte!" Kara swatted her daughter's arm.

Charlotte turned to Ethan, stage-whispering, "Mom needs to get out more, you know."

"I get out plenty, thank you very much," Kara said, feeling a blush creep up her cheeks.

"Sure, Mom. Whatever you say." Charlotte grinned, heading toward the door. "Love you, Mom! Have fun on your *not-date*!" she called over her shoulder, disappearing before Kara could respond.

Ethan laughed. "She's quite the character."

Kara sighed, shaking her head. "That she is."

"So," Ethan said, "what do you say? Want to join me at Phil's tonight? For old times' sake?"

Kara's heart pounded as she found her head bobbling. "Yeah? Yeah. Sure. Of course. Why not? That sounds nice. What time?"

Ethan chuckled. "How about I pick you up at seven?"

"Works for me," Kara replied, her voice slightly higher than usual. "See you then."

As Ethan walked out, Kara stood there, heart pounding, her mind racing to catch up. She'd agreed to dinner with him—just like that.

How did I let that happen?

And more importantly, what am I gonna wear?

16

Ethan

ETHAN CLOSED THE FRONT door, and Hero bounded down the hallway, paws skidding on the smooth floor.

"Hey buddy! Miss me?" Ethan chuckled, bending down to ruffle the fur on Hero's neck.

"I know, I know. Come on, let's go outside."

Hero didn't need to be told twice. He darted past Ethan and through the doggy door, while Ethan ambled to the kitchen. At the counter, Ethan grabbed a tennis ball from the mesh bag full of dog toys before stepping onto the back porch and shielding his eyes against the afternoon sun.

Hero's eyes lit up, and his fluffy tail wagged wildly when Ethan revealed the worn, neon-yellow tennis ball. With a grin, Ethan tossed the ball across the yard, watching as Hero bounded after it with unbridled enthusiasm, his paws kicking up tufts of grass.

As Hero raced back with the ball, Ethan's mind wandered to the rescue, and inevitably, to Kara. He couldn't help but marvel at Kara's dedication. The sheer amount of work she managed on her own was staggering. Hero dropped the ball, now coated in slobber, at Ethan's feet, tail swishing back and forth.

"Good boy," Ethan praised, picking up the ball and throwing it again. He smiled as he watched Hero chase after it and recalled his night with Kara. It had been good to hang out with her again, even if it was more work related. There was something about her presence that made even the most mundane tasks enjoyable.

His mind shifted to Charlotte, and a chuckle escaped as he remembered her quick wit. She reminded him so much of Kara—the same warmth in her smile, the same determination in her eyes when she set her mind to something. The apple hadn't fallen far from the tree.

Ethan headed inside after a few more throws, Hero trotting close behind. "Come on, boy. Let's get you something to eat."

In the kitchen, the sound of kibble hitting the metal bowl filled the air as Ethan prepared Hero's dinner and refreshed his water. He watched the dog eat, his thoughts returning to Kara and the rescue. There had to be other ways he could help lighten her load.

Wait. I got it.

Ethan hurried down the hallway, his footsteps muffled by the faded carpet runner. Entering the bedroom, Hero trotted in after him, his collar jingling with each step.

"Keeping me company?" Ethan smiled, reaching down to give Hero a quick scratch behind the ears.

He cleared off the weathered oak desk, dumping the haphazard piles of books and overstuffed folders onto the twin bed. Sitting in the swivel chair, he opened the center drawer and pulled out a notebook and a pen. As he did, he felt Hero's warm presence against his leg, the dog having inched closer to rest his head on Ethan's foot.

For the next few hours, Ethan scribbled furiously, his pen flying across the paper, jotting down ideas from his time at the Virginia rescue, the scratching sound filling the quiet room. Every now and then, Ethan paused, twirling the pen between his fingers as he thought. Some things he had written down were strategies that had worked well, others were plans they'd never had the chance to implement. But he wasn't sure if Kara had tried any of these before, and it couldn't hurt to share them with her.

He reached down, giving Hero a gentle pat.

"What do you think, boy?" Ethan asked. "Think Kara will like these ideas?"

Hero responded with a soft woof and a thump of his tail against the floor, which Ethan chose to interpret as a yes.

The fading afternoon light caught Ethan's attention. His phone screen glowed: 6:25 p.m.

"Shoot, I need to get ready," he muttered, scrambling to his feet. As he did, a thought crossed his mind.

Is this ... a date?

The word *date* hung in his mind. Ethan shook his head, as if trying to dislodge the thought.

"It's not. I mean, we're ..." Ethan trailed off, shaking his head. "Catching up, that's all."

But even as he tried to convince himself, a small smile tugged at the corners of his mouth. Date or not, Ethan couldn't deny the flutter in his chest at the thought of seeing Kara again.

With that warmth still lingering in his chest, Ethan moved to his bag, rummaging through his clothes. "Just hanging out," he repeated to himself, even as he bypassed his usual t-shirts in favor of something nicer.

After a moment of deliberation, he pulled out a crisp, light blue button-down shirt, the faint scent of laundry detergent still clinging to the fabric, and a pair of dark wash jeans with a slight fade at the knees. He held the shirt up against himself, examining his reflection in the mirror.

"Rate my outfit, Hero," Ethan said, turning to the dog who had made himself comfortable on the twin bed, sprawled out among the books and folders Ethan had dumped there.

Hero's tail thumped against a stack of papers, scattering a few to the floor.

"Solid eight, huh? What do I have to do to get a ten?" Ethan chuckled, striking a mock pose.

Hero tilted his head, letting out a soft whine.

"Oh, come on. Don't give me that look. This is my best shirt. Well, the best option I have tonight. Isn't that a factor?"

The dog responded by rolling onto his back, paws in the air, tongue lolling out.

"All right, all right." Ethan laughed, reaching over to rub Hero's belly. "I get it. The outfit's fine, but it's my personality that matters more, right?"

Hero's tail wagged furiously in response.

"You're a good wingman, you know that?" Ethan said,

giving Hero one last pat before turning back to the mirror.

As he buttoned up the shirt, smoothing out the collar, Ethan caught sight of his reflection. He grimaced, running a hand through his unruly hair. It had grown longer than usual, and now it seemed intent on sticking up in all directions.

Ethan grabbed a comb from the dresser, its teeth catching as he attempted to tame his unruly hair into some semblance of order. After a few minutes, he got it looking reasonably presentable.

"Not bad," he said, angling his head to check his handiwork from different sides.

As he reached inside the bag for his belt, his hand brushed against something unexpected, and he retrieved a small bottle of cologne he'd forgotten he'd packed. It had been ages since he'd worn any, but something made him pause.

When he turned the bottle over, a faint smile curved his lips as he recognized the familiar label—the same brand he'd started using back in high school.

With a shrug, he dabbed a bit on his neck and wrists. Ethan closed his eyes, the scent pulling him back to the very first time he'd ever worn that cologne ...

***

"Why do you smell so good?" Kara asked, gliding by Ethan with the mop.

Ethan slid a box of supplies onto the shelf, grinning. "Just something new I'm trying out." He stretched his back, brushing his hands on his khakis before turning to face her.

"Want me to finish mopping?"

Kara raised an eyebrow. "You, offering to mop? Now that's new." She shook her head with a smile. "I'm nearly done. Did you remember to take out the trash?"

"Already done."

Kara propped the mop against the wall with a soft clunk and slipped a hair tie off her wrist. "Is it just me, or is it stuffy in here?" She fanned her face with one hand. "Dad needs to stop cutting off the AC when we close. We're still working for like an hour after that."

As she gathered her chestnut hair into a messy bun, Ethan couldn't look away from her effortless grace. Even in her simple Walker's Pharmacy uniform—an oversized t-shirt, wrinkled khakis, and scuffed sneakers—she radiated a beauty that took his breath away.

The air between them crackled with electricity. His pulse quickened, each beat echoing in his ears as he took a single, tentative step toward her.

The moment stretched out between them. Ethan knew some silences spoke louder than words, and this one was screaming everything his heart had been trying to say that entire summer.

"Missed one," he said, his fingers gently brushing her cheek as he tucked an errant strand of hair behind her ear.

Kara's eyes, warm pools of amber flecked with gold, locked onto his gaze, a mixture of amusement and desire dancing in their depths. "Was that really about my hair," she whispered, "or did you just want an excuse to get closer?"

Ethan's lips quirked into a half-smile. "Should I back

off?"

Kara's fingers curled into the fabric of his shirt, pulling him closer. "Don't you dare," she murmured, tilting her chin upward. "Kiss me."

⁓

KNOCK. KNOCK. KNOCK.

Hero's ears shot up, and he bolted toward the front door.

"Hold on, boy," Ethan called out, setting down the cologne and following Hero to the entryway.

Ethan glanced at his phone as he approached the door. *At 6:30?*

Curious, he peered through the window. A stocky man in a stained uniform stood on the porch, and behind him, a white van with *Locksmith* emblazoned on its side was parked in the cracked driveway.

Ethan opened the door, his other hand on Hero's collar to keep him from rushing out.

"Locksmith service. You called about a safe?" the man asked, gesturing with his toolbox.

"Yeah, that's right. Come on in," Ethan said, stepping aside to let the locksmith enter.

"Sorry for the delay. Got caught up with some emergency calls earlier."

"No problem." Ethan said. "It was my dad's. He passed away and I can't find the key."

"Alright, lead the way," the locksmith replied, picking up his toolbox.

Ethan led the locksmith to his dad's bedroom. As they

entered, he pointed to the oak dresser against the far wall. "There it is."

The locksmith approached, toolbox clinking as he set it on the floor. He ran his hand over the safe's surface, studying it closely before letting out a low whistle. "This is an older model, all right. Maybe thirty years old? Don't let that fool you, though. These things were built to last—and to keep people out."

Great.

Ethan nodded, retreating to give him space. He sat down on the bed and watched as the locksmith pulled out a couple of different tools.

"I'll start with the drill," the locksmith explained. "Fair warning—it might scratch up the safe a bit. That okay with you?"

Ethan shrugged. "Go for it. I don't care about the safe—it's what's inside that matters."

What I hope's inside.

Ethan held his breath as the sound of the drill on the keyhole reverberated around the room. His foot tapped and his stomach tightened while the locksmith struggled.

Come on, come on. Open already!

The locksmith frowned, setting the drill aside. "Tough one. Didn't even scratch it. Let's try something else."

Ethan watched, nerves fraying like an old rope, as the locksmith delicately maneuvered the tool inside the keyhole. The man's forehead creased, beads of sweat forming at his temples.

Ethan checked his phone again: 6:45 p.m.

In his mind, he could already hear Kara's voice. "Running late again, Ethan?" He swallowed hard, his throat dry as sandpaper, racking his brain for an excuse that would sound better than the one he had given earlier.

Please hurry for the love of—

"No luck. Not with any of the tools I got, anyway," the locksmith said, wiping his brow.

Ethan's shoulders sagged. "Now what?"

"I'll need to order some specialized equipment. Could take a couple weeks to arrive, though."

"Fine, do it. Just as soon as possible, please."

"You got it. I'll call you as soon as they're in," the locksmith assured him, packing up his tools.

Ethan barely heard him, already rushing him out the door, glancing at his phone: 6:48 p.m.

Can't be late.

He rushed to slip on his shoes, then darted to the kitchen and grabbed the pill bottle off the counter, frowning.

Only one left after this.

Ethan pulled out his phone and fired off a quick email to his psychiatrist's office:

Dr. Hartman,

Where did you send my new prescription? Didn't get an update. I'm down to my last pill.

Thanks,
  Ethan

He swallowed the pill with a gulp of water, then patted his

pockets.

Wallet. Where's my wallet?

Ethan spun around, scanning the counters. There it was, right next to where the pill bottle had been. He snatched it up, shoving it into his back pocket.

"Hero! Gotta run. I'll be back later, buddy!" he called out.

Hero trotted over and Ethan kneeled quickly, giving him a quick kiss on the head. "Be a good boy, okay?"

Just as Ethan reached the front door, he halted.

The notebook.

Spinning on his heel for what he hoped was the final time, he rushed back to his bedroom, grabbed the notebook from the bed, and tucked it under his arm. With one last glance at his phone—6:52 p.m.—Ethan dashed out the door, praying he'd make it to Kara's on time.

17

Kara

Kara stepped out onto the gravel driveway, the crunch beneath her sandals sounding sharp in the quiet as Ethan's truck rolled to a stop.

He hopped down from the driver's seat, his boots hitting the ground with a soft thud, and strode over to the passenger door.

Taking a deep breath, Kara broke the ice first. "Wow, you actually made it on time. I'm impressed." She paused, then added with a chuckle, "too soon?"

"Nah, it's never too soon." A sheepish grin spread across Ethan's face. "Also, I think we both know I had that coming."

Kara shifted under Ethan's gaze, smoothing her light blue sundress, the cotton soft beneath her fingers as the warm evening breeze teased the hem.

As if reading her thoughts, Ethan's eyes traveled over her outfit. "You look absolutely gorgeous."

Kara's breath caught in her throat, a warm flutter spreading through her chest, and she too found herself momentarily stunned by Ethan's appearance—the light blue button-up shirt hugging his broad shoulders, tucked neatly into dark wash jeans that tapered down to his boots.

"Thanks. You clean up pretty nice yourself." She grinned and gestured to his hair. "Getting some serious *Top Gun* vibes there, Maverick."

Ethan's blue eyes glinted as he leaned slightly toward her. "Well, if I'm Maverick, does that make you my Goose? Well, minus the part where Goose, you know ..."

The quip sent a little spark through Kara, but before she could respond, he swung open the passenger door with a playful bow and offered his hand. "Need help getting up?"

"I think I can manage, thanks." She hoisted herself up into the seat, trying to ignore the butterflies in her stomach as Ethan closed the door and rounded the truck.

A faint trace of Ethan's old cologne lingered in the air—spice with an afternote of wood and a hint of something warm like amber. It was the same scent he used to wear all those years ago. Her eyes roamed over the dashboard, taking in the worn steering wheel and the old coffee stain on the center console. It was as if time had barely touched the truck, and yet, so much had changed between them.

Ethan started the engine and pulled away from the curb before turning down the radio. "So, yeah, how's your day been?"

Kara turned to him with a smirk. "Um, you do remember spending most of it with me, right?"

"Yeah, yeah. I meant after I left. What'd you do?"

Kara shrugged, fingers toying with the hem of her dress. "Oh, you know, the glamorous life of a rescue owner. Sorting through endless vet bills, brainstorming for the next adoption event, and trying to find enough donations to keep the lights on. Living the dream." She glanced at him. "What about you? Any earth-shattering developments since this afternoon?"

Ethan drummed his fingers on the steering wheel. "No, nothing really."

"I guess no news is good news, right?" Kara gestured toward the stereo. "Mind if I change it?"

"Yeah, sure. Go for it."

Kara reached for the stereo, pressing play on the CD that was already in. Her eyes widened as familiar notes filled the truck. "No way! Is this what I think it is?"

"Yep, that's the one. Our infamous mix CD. It's kind of been a permanent fixture in here over the years."

Kara burst into laughter. "I can't believe you kept this! Remember our Limewire marathons? Hours of downloading, praying we wouldn't destroy your computer?"

"How could I forget? Pretty sure my computer is still recovering from all those viruses. Worth it, though."

As they cruised down the familiar streets, the opening notes of a song drifted from the speakers. The gentle guitar strums and soft vocals transported Kara back to their first date—she could almost feel the warmth of Ethan's hands on her waist as they swayed to this melody.

More memories rushed in—stargazing in the bed of this truck after late pharmacy shifts, sneaking out to the beach, sharing hopes and dreams in whispered conversations. This blue Chevy had been a place where two teenagers in love could escape the world. But the last memory struck her—a promise Ethan never kept.

Kara shook her head slightly, pushing the thought away.

Before she knew it, Ethan was pulling into the parking lot of Phil's Diner.

They climbed out and made their way inside. Ethan held the door open for her as Phil's booming voice carried across the diner. "Well, look what the cat dragged in. Good to see you kids!"

"Hey, Phil." Kara waved, casting a side glance at the diner full of patrons. "Anything open for us?"

Phil jerked his thumb toward a booth by the window. "Got a spot right there. Give me a sec, and I'll bring y'all some menus."

Ethan nodded, leading the way over. Kara sat down first with her back toward the rest of the diner. Ethan slid in across from her.

Phil bustled over, his round belly preceding him, and the menus tucked under one arm. "Here we go." He slapped the laminated menus down on the table with a practiced flourish. "What'll it be for drinks?"

"Sweet tea would be great," Ethan said.

Kara glanced up from her menu. "Make that two. Thanks, Phil."

Phil nodded and turned on his heel, heading back to the kitchen.

What if I spill something on my dress? Ugh, I should've ordered water ... but water's free and then he might think things are worse than they are. They aren't great though ... but not that bad either. Okay, just breathe.

Kara turned her attention to the menu, her eyes drifting over the words without really reading them.

Right, what's light, healthy and won't make Ethan think I eat too much or make me look like I need rolling out of here when we're done.

She stared at the menu, her gaze glazing over its contents.

Kara chuckled, shaking her head. "Why am I even pretending to read this? Pretty sure I could recite it in my sleep by now."

Ethan leaned back with a wry smile. "Tell me about it. Not much has changed since the last time we—"

Phil returned, holding two glasses of sweet tea. "All right, here you go," he said, setting the drinks down with a clink. He wiped his hands on his apron and pulled out a notepad. "Ready to order?"

Kara hesitated, then said, "You know what? I'll just stick with some fries for now, thanks."

"Hmm." Ethan looked up from his menu. "Actually, I'm gonna try one of those Beyond Cheesesteak subs with fries, please."

Kara perked up. "I had one yesterday. It was insanely good." With a quick nod toward Phil, she added, "I'll have the Beyond Cheesesteak too, but with extra banana peppers, please."

Phil scribbled on his notepad, nodding. "You got it. Those things have been flying outta the kitchen lately." He collected their menus and headed to the back.

Kara took a sip of her sweet tea as Ethan reached into his

pocket.

"Um, so, there's something I wanted to tell you," he said.

Kara found her breath trapped in her throat, her heart racing. "Oh?"

"Well, I'll be! If it isn't the town's favorite couple!" a familiar, shrill voice rang out.

Kara turned and plastered on a smile, her tone overly bright. "Ada! How've you been?"

Of course she'd be here.

Ada's heavily mascaraed eyes darted between them like a spectator at a tennis match. "Oh, not nearly as good as you two lovebirds, I bet!" She turned to Ethan, patting his shoulder with a bejeweled hand. "And Ethan, honey, you're as dashing as ever." Her gaze swiveled to Kara, eyebrows raised suggestively. "Wouldn't you agree, Kara?"

Heat crept up Kara's neck. "Oh, um, actually Ada, we were in the middle of—"

"Oh, don't you try to be coy with me!" Ada continued, cutting her off. "It's so nice to see young people getting back together in Hadley Cove. Our very own Romeo and Juliet."

Kara inwardly groaned, then opened her mouth, but nothing came out. There was no getting out of this now.

Ethan quirked an eyebrow and leaned in, "You know, Ada, I'm not sure about the Romeo and Juliet comparison. Didn't end too well for them, if I recall."

Kara stifled a snort.

Ada waved off Ethan's comment, undeterred. "Oh, details, details. The point is, it's just delightful to see you two together again." She leaned in conspiratorially. "Say, have you heard about Lisa and Noah's summer special at the Sandy Shores Inn? It's all over the Facebook. Perfect for couples, you know. I could give Lisa a quick text, see if she can squeeze you in. Frank and I just adore it there. And don't even get me started on their muffins—"

Phil's voice cut through the chatter, making her jump. "Pardon me, Ada!" He skillfully maneuvered around her with two heaping plates. "Got some hungry customers here waiting on their dinner."

"Oh! Of course, of course." She shuffled to the side, eyes still fixed on Kara and Ethan. "Don't let me keep you from your romantic dinner!"

Phil set the plates down. "Voila! Two Beyond Cheesesteaks, loaded with all the fixings, and a mountain of our world-famous fries. Bon appétit, you two!"

"Thanks, Phil," Kara and Ethan chimed simultaneously. Their eyes met over the steaming plates, and they shared a small, amused smile at their synchronicity.

Ada beamed at them one last time. "Well, I'll let you two lovebirds enjoy your meal in peace. Don't do anything I wouldn't do!" She winked before finally retreating to the counter.

A silence settled between them as Ethan picked up his sub, but he paused, glancing at Kara with a mischievous glint in his eyes. "Well, if we're the town's lovebirds, I guess we should at least give them a show, right?"

"Ethan, stop," she laughed, swatting at his arm. "You're terrible."

He wiggled his eyebrows dramatically and leaned in slightly, lowering his voice as if they were about to be up to no good. "Terrible? I think you mean terribly charming."

She picked up a fry from his plate, swatting the bridge of his nose with it. "Terribly something, all right."

Ethan grinned, settling back in his seat, and then blinked. "Hey, that one was mine. Hear ye, hear ye, we have a fry thief."

"What an accusation! I do not steal fries. I merely ... re-distribute them for the greater good."

"Ah, of course. Robin Hood of the diner booth."

Kara popped one of his fries into her mouth, grinning. "See? This isn't awkward at all."

Ethan winked, then took a huge bite of his sub. A smear of sauce clung to the corner of his mouth as he mumbled around his mouthful, "Oh man, you weren't kidding. This is so good."

Kara picked up her own sandwich, taking a more delicate bite. Her eyes closed briefly as she savored the flavors ... Swallowing, she nodded appreciatively. "Mm, you know what? It's even better than yesterday. How's that even pos-sible?"

"It's possible, then again could just be the company." Ethan gave her a soft smile, his eyes holding hers for a mo-ment longer than usual.

Kara's breath hitched for just a second and she quickly broke eye contact, reaching for her napkin as if to distract herself. Clearing her throat, she set the sandwich down. "So, before Hurricane Ada blew through, you were about to tell me something?"

"Oh, right!" He sipped his tea then fished out some folded papers from his pocket. "I, uh, I've been thinking about your rescue. Had some ideas that might help drum up more interest in adoptions."

Kara stared at the papers. "You did all this?

Ethan rubbed the back of his neck, suddenly looking a bit self-conscious. "Yeah, I hope you don't mind. I know I'm still pretty new to your setup, and you've been running the show for ages. But I picked up some tricks at that rescue in Virginia, and I thought maybe some of those ideas could work here too."

This gesture was the last thing she'd expected. "Can I see what you've come up with?"

"Yeah, of course." Ethan pushed the papers toward her, his finger tracing over different sections. "So, up here, that's just me throwing ideas at the wall. But down here, these are some strategies that worked for us back in Virginia."

Kara's eyes scanned the page. "Hold on, what's this about? 'Picture day'?"

"Oh, that. When I started volunteering, I was on dog grooming duty. Then I thought, once the pups are all spruced up, why not show them off? So, I set up a photo area outside, got them in the sunlight, and snapped some pictures. Then we put them on the website." He tapped the paper. "I've outlined the process here—ideas for backdrops, props, and a schedule to rotate the animals through grooming and photo sessions."

Kara's mouth dropped as she took in the level of detail.

Ethan's eyes lit up as he continued. "You wouldn't believe the difference it made. Adoptions skyrocketed, and kennels emptied fast. We built an entire crew—groomers, photographers, everyone pitched in for 'picture days.' And it even cut costs—fewer long-term residents meant lower overhead. Total win-win."

Kara blinked, her vision swimming as she struggled to process the sheer volume of thought and effort spread across the pages before her.

He flipped to the next page, revealing a sea of notes. "Here are social media ideas to showcase the photos, thoughts on partnering with local businesses for sponsorships, and I even drafted a startup budget to get things rolling."

A lump formed in her throat, making her voice crack when she finally spoke. "Ethan," she breathed, her fingers hovering over the paper as if it might disappear, "you did all of this for my rescue?"

Ethan's voice softened, his eyes meeting hers. "Yeah, I did. For the animals, of course, but also ..." he hesitated, then finished quietly, "for you."

She blinked back tears and took a deep breath. "This is incredible. You've thought of *everything*. You put so much time and effort into this." Kara's gaze lifted from the papers to meet Ethan's eyes. "This could change everything for Second Chance. I-I don't know what to say."

Ethan reached out, gently placing his hand over hers. "You don't have to say anything."

Kara squeezed Ethan's hand as if it were a lifeline. "Thank you. You have no idea how much this means to me. How much it means to the animals."

"It's nothing, really." Ethan shrugged. "Just a few suggestions that might help things. You've already done such an awesome job with the place."

"Well," Kara's smile faltered, "it was great at first, yeah. But lately we've been hitting some rough patches. These past few months have been—" She paused, her voice dropping. "I couldn't bring myself to tell anyone. It felt like I was failing the animals. I—"

Ethan's grip on her hand tightened. "You can tell me anything, Kara. No judgment. Ever."

Anything? Is he sure? No, he doesn't mean it ... Does he?

Kara drew in a shaky breath, quickly brushing away a tear. "I mean, you've pretty much seen the highlight reel already. Not enough volunteers. The kennels are full, and I'm drowning in never-ending tasks. I was barely treading water until—" She met his eyes. "Until you showed up."

Ethan nodded, a determined look settling on his face. "All right, here's what we're gonna do. Let's break this down, figure out our top priorities. We'll tackle this one step at a time, okay? You've got this, Kara."

As they discussed potential solutions and strategies, Kara felt a sense of hope growing. Time seemed to blur as they went over every detail, bouncing ideas back and forth.

At some point, Kara reached for her drink, tilting the glass only to find a trickle of watery tea and a few melted ice cubes sliding toward her lips. She set it down, her fingers leaving marks in the condensation. Her gaze dropped to her plate, where the pile of fries had dwindled to three stragglers.

Across the table, Ethan's plate mirrored her own. Crumbs from his sub dotted the empty space, and a lone fry lay abandoned next to a small puddle of ketchup. His tea glass stood empty, a ring of moisture marking its place on the table.

To Kara, time had always been their enemy, but tonight,

it felt like an old friend. "Ethan, this is amazing. I feel like we've mapped out a whole new future for the rescue in just one dinner."

"You've built something incredible already. Now we're just fine-tuning it." Ethan smiled, checking his phone before sliding some bills onto the table.

Kara's hand instinctively went to her purse. "Oh, let me chip in—"

"Don't worry about it. It's on me."

Kara felt a flutter in her chest at his gesture. It was such a small thing, but it felt significant somehow.

Ethan rose from his seat, arching his back in a stretch. "Well, I hate to say it, but we should probably think about heading out. You good to go?"

Kara nodded, though her heart sank a little. "Yeah, I suppose so," she said, unable to keep a small sigh from escaping.

Does this night have to end?

18

Ethan

ETHAN TURNED THE KEY again, pumping the gas pedal as if willing the truck to roar to life. No luck.

He let out a breath and looked at Kara. "Could be the battery. I'll get out and look."

With a resigned sigh, Ethan reached for the door handle. As he eased out of the driver's seat and lifted the creaking hood, the soft thud of the passenger door echoed behind him.

A few seconds later, Kara appeared at his side.

"Hey, you don't have to get out. I'll only be a sec," Ethan said, glancing back at Kara.

Kara shrugged. "It's no big deal. Besides, who'd be your trusty flashlight holder?" She flicked on her phone's flashlight.

"Fair enough. Just, uh, watch out for the grease. Don't want it to get on that pretty dress of yours."

Or pretty you.

"Please, I'm always covered in something—dog hair, mud, you name it. But thanks for the consideration." Kara edged closer, her arm brushing his. "This work for you?"

Ethan swallowed hard. "Yeah, uh, perfect. Thanks."

Kara moved closer, peering into the engine. "So, what's your diagnosis? Battery issue, or something else?"

Ethan's eyes flicked to the battery, but his focus lingered on her. "Oh, uh ... Yeah. Pretty sure it's the battery."

Kara turned, her face only inches from his, lowering the flashlight. "Are you sure?" Her voice softened, barely above a whisper.

Ethan's breath caught in his throat as he met her gaze. He swallowed, nodding slowly. "Uh, I think so."

In that moment, as their eyes locked, the years between them melted away like snow in springtime. Then the world around him seemed to fade, leaving just the two of them. The space between them shrank, and her lips parted slightly.

His heartbeat thundered in his ears, every muscle in his body tightened, drawn to her like gravity. All he could think about was closing the distance, but he didn't. He hovered there, inches away, his gaze on her—waiting, wanting.

BEEP! BEEP!

Instinct kicked in before thought, and Ethan stepped in front of Kara, one arm extended as he shielded her from the sudden noise. His hand brushed her shoulder, steadying her as he glanced around.

Kara blinked, dazed, her arms crossing over her chest. "What was that?"

Ethan turned, heart still racing, right in time to see his old neighbor pulling up beside them. The tension in his shoulders eased, but his arm lingered near Kara, as if reluctant to let the moment slip.

"You all right there, Ethan?" Clyde called out. Jumping out of his truck, he walked over to them. "Car trouble?"

Ethan's pulse hammered, but he forced a smile. "Yeah … something like that. Appreciate you stopping."

Clyde winked. "Don't go thanking me yet. I haven't fixed a dern thing."

Kara stepped back as Clyde made his way over to look under the hood.

"Dead battery?" he asked.

Ethan shrugged. "I think so. It was working fine earlier—"

"No worry there. I've got jumper cables in my cab." Clyde walked back over to his truck.

Ethan glanced over at Kara, giving her a sympathetic smile. She let out a chuckle, pulling her phone back out as Clyde came back with the cables.

"All right, you wanna hook those up, Ethan?" Clyde asked, holding out the two cables.

"Of course." He grabbed the cables from Clyde's hand and hooked them up to his battery.

"Let me start 'er up," Clyde said. "Then you can give yours a go."

Kara turned off her phone's flashlight and leaned against the side of Phil's Diner.

"You want to wait in the truck?" Ethan asked, opening the driver's side door.

Kara shook her head. "No, it's okay. I'm good here."

"Alright. Hopefully we can get going soon." Ethan climbed into the truck and waited. After hearing Clyde's truck roar to life next to him, he held his breath and turned the key. The truck turned on like clockwork. Breathing a sigh of relief, Ethan jumped out of the truck and unhooked the cables.

"Thanks a million, Clyde. Really." He handed the jumper cables back.

"Not a problem at all. And you get that little lady home safe, you hear?" Clyde pointed at Kara.

Ethan nodded. "Will do. Thanks again."

As Clyde's taillights disappeared down the road, a gentle silence settled over the parking lot. Ethan and Kara stood as if they were each waiting for the other to say something first.

"Uh, should we get going?" Kara asked. "Now that the truck is running?"

Ethan nodded and circled to the passenger side. "Of course. Let me get your door," he said, opening the door as Kara approached. Offering his hand, he helped her up into the seat, then gently closed the door behind her before hurrying back to his side and sliding into the driver's seat. Ethan fired up the engine, and they pulled onto the road.

—ele—

Stars twinkled like scattered diamonds over Hadley Cove as they cruised down Main Street. Wisps of clouds, barely visible, floated across the deep indigo sky. They passed the market, its windows shimmering with the warm glow of the streetlights, while the brass fixtures of Hadley Cove Savings & Loan glinted in the moonlight.

"Hey, there's the old ice cream place," Ethan pointed out. "You still like butter pecan?"

"Of course—it's the only flavor worth getting. Charlotte loves it too. It's her favorite."

"She's her mother's daughter," Ethan said, smiling at Kara.

She gave him a small smile, then looked away. "And there's the old pizza place."

"Do their pies still taste like cardboard?" Ethan asked.

"Unfortunately, yes," Kara said with a chuckle. "Don't know how they're still in business."

"Well, if they're still the only pizza place in town, I guess folks don't have a choice. It's cardboard or nothing."

Kara chuckled. "They still are. But I seem to remember you eating a slice or two."

"Only because I was sharing it with you," Ethan said, turning onto a road that went along the water.

Kara didn't reply, but Ethan could see that she was smiling as she rolled down her window, leaning out to let the breeze catch her outstretched hand.

Seven minutes later, they pulled up in front of Kara's tiny house. Ethan's hand moved to the door handle, ready to step out into the night. But before he could make a move, Kara reached out, her fingers brushing his arm.

"You don't have to walk me to the door, Ethan."

"Yes, I do." He hopped out and jogged over to her door, opening it. "Old habits, you know."

Kara nodded, taking his hand as she got out. "That was a

long time ago."

"It was," Ethan said, walking up the stone path to her porch.

"Well," Kara turned to him, taking her keys out of her purse, "I had a nice time tonight."

"So did I," Ethan told her, though his voice came out quieter than he expected. He didn't want the night to end—not after what almost happened. He had been so close to her. So close.

And now it's over.

Kara smiled, but there was something in her eyes that made Ethan pause.

Is she hesitating? ... Is she thinking about ... Should I say something and break the silence, or leave it for another night?

For a brief second, it looked as if she might say something more, something that could bring them back to the moment before Clyde interrupted. But instead, she fidgeted with her keys.

"Should I come by tomorrow?" Ethan asked, though it felt like such a small thing to say after everything that almost was.

Kara nodded. "Sounds good."

Another silence stretched between them.

Ethan shifted his weight, unsure of what to say next, his eyes wandering to the small porch behind her. The driftwood loveseat, weathered but inviting, caught his attention first, surrounded by hanging ferns that swayed gently in the breeze. A whimsical wind chime made of colorful sea glass tinkled softly, catching glints of starlight. He could almost picture her there, in the quiet of the evening, barefoot and sipping sweet tea as she stargazed, always keeping one ear out for her rescue animals.

The whole setup had a cozy, intimate feel—simple yet full of life, like Kara. It made him want to stay longer, say something more to fill the silence. But what?

Just say something. Anything.

Ethan opened his mouth to say something, but nothing came out. The words were stuck tangled in a mess of emotions he couldn't explain. His hand twitched at his side, wanting to reach for her, to hold on to whatever it was they had rekindled tonight.

Kara, wait ... The thought came, but his voice didn't follow. He wanted to say her name, to stop her from leaving, but the words remained stuck within him.

Before he could gather himself, she turned to the door, fiddling with the lock. And just like that, the moment was gone.

"Um, well, good night," Kara said.

"Yeah. Good night."

Sticking his hands in his pockets, Ethan waited until she unlocked the door and went inside, then walked back to his truck.

As he pulled away from Kara's house, the soft glow of her porch light faded in his rearview mirror. Driving through town, Ethan's thoughts kept returning to her—the easy conversation over dinner, her laugh echoing in the warm evening air, and that particular smile that had always made his heart skip. Then there was that moment—breathless and suspended in time—when he'd leaned in, drawn to her by an irresistible pull. Kara had tilted her face up, her eyes fluttering shut. He could almost feel the warmth of her lips, just a heartbeat away.

What if Clyde hadn't shown up?

Ethan sighed, the memory of their almost-kiss replaying in slow motion—equal parts regret and longing. But as he rounded the corner and passed Walker's Pharmacy, the thought evaporated, and his stomach twisted, dragging him back to the last time he'd set foot there ...

Ethan parked his truck outside Walker's Pharmacy and hopped out. Last night, his phone had slipped from his grip, sinking into the ocean—lost to the currents forever. He'd promised Kara he would call her today, but now all he had was an empty pocket and a sense of urgency to replace the phone before she thought he'd forgotten. With a sigh, he squared his shoulders, hoping Mr. Walker might be in a generous enough mood to advance his paycheck a few days.

As Ethan neared the entrance, something felt wrong. There, hunched before the door, stood Whitaker Walker—or rather, a shadow of the man Ethan remembered. Gone was the crisp white coat and neatly combed hair. Instead, a rumpled shirt clung to his thin frame, and bruises bloomed in sickly purples and yellows across his skin.

Mr. Walker's trembling hands—hands that looked far older than they should—fumbled with a piece of paper as he tried to tape it to the door.

As Ethan drew closer, the scrawled words came into focus: *Closed Until Further Notice.*

"Mr. Walker?" Ethan's voice came out softer than intended. "What's going on? You all right?"

The pharmacist's head snapped around at the sound. For a heartbeat, he seemed not to recognize Ethan, but then he lunged with a speed that belied his disheveled state.

Ethan barely had time to react before Mr. Walker grabbed his shirt, slamming him into the brick wall. The breath rushed out of his lungs, leaving him gasping.

"Hey! What the—" Ethan wheezed, hands scrabbling to break free of the older man's iron grip.

Bloodshot eyes, rimmed with red, locked onto Ethan's. Grief and fury twisted Mr. Walker's face into something unrecognizable—something darker. "It's your fault! You killed her. If you hadn't—"

19

Kara

TWISTING HER CHESTNUT HAIR into a loose bun, Kara stepped out of her bedroom, swapping the dress for her favorite worn jeans, a band t-shirt, and a pair of scuffed once-white sneakers. But as she moved around her tiny home, searching for the rescue's keys to do her nightly check, she couldn't help but think about the evening she'd had with Ethan, and how happy it had made her feel.

Her mind wandered to their almost-kiss. A small part of her was relieved it didn't happen, though she couldn't quite figure out why. They'd been here before, all those years ago. The pain of what came after still lingered in her chest, a reminder that some things were better left in the past. However, as his lips had parted ever so slightly, his breath warm against her skin, all she could think about was how much she missed him. How much she wanted to forget the past and just—feel.

Yet, despite the emotions swirling inside her, there was

something new—a sense of calm, of comfort. Maybe it was the way Ethan had offered more than memories—a future for her rescue, for her.

Kara smiled, appreciating how thoughtful Ethan had been in helping her draw up a plan for the rescue. Even if it didn't work out exactly as they hoped, his willingness to put in the effort meant the world to her. And with the rescue's future on the line, any plan seemed worth exploring.

After finding her keys buried beneath newspapers on the kitchen table, Kara walked over to the door, smirking as she remembered something funny that Ethan had said.

"Mom!" Charlotte called, bursting through the door.

Kara jumped. "Geez, Charlotte!" She laughed, jingling her keys. "I was just heading out to check on the—"

Charlotte raised a hand. "Whoa there, Super Mom. You don't need to go over there."

"I don't?"

"Already took care of it," Charlotte said with a proud grin. "Checks done, dogs had their last potty break. Everything's sorted. You can chill tonight."

"Wow, really?" Kara's face softened into a grateful smile as she tossed her keys onto the counter. "Thanks, honey. You're a lifesaver."

Charlotte beamed, then chuckled. "Oh, I know. But get this—Pepper went to town on his new blanket. Chewed a massive hole right in the middle and stuck his head through it. You should've seen him."

"Oh no, not the brand new one? Are you serious?"

"Yeah, but don't freak out. I got a picture. You've gotta see this—it's too cute."

Charlotte pulled out her phone and showed Kara the photo. They both leaned in, looking at the image of Pepper, the Jack Russel terrier mix's furry face framed by the ragged hole in the blanket, tongue lolling out in a doggy grin.

Kara's hand drifted to her chest. "Oh my heart, he's adorable. Did you get him another blanket?"

Charlotte gasped. "Mom! What do you take me for? Of course, our little destroyer gets all the blankets he wants."

Kara chuckled, then sighed. "We're gonna go broke replacing blankets at this rate." She turned and grabbed the kettle from the stove, filling it up at the sink. "Did you want some tea?"

"I'm good, thanks," Charlotte said, flopping onto the nearby couch. She leaned forward. "So, spill. How was the big date?"

"It wasn't a date. Just dinner." Kara focused on pulling out a mug and getting a tea bag ready.

"Oh, come on, Mom. You can tell me about your date. I'm not a kid anymore."

"And I'm telling you, it wasn't a date."

"Uh-huh, sure, whatever you say." Charlotte snickered, reaching for her phone. "Anyway, I'm heading out. Friends are doing a beach thing."

"This late? Thought you were staying in tonight."

Charlotte stood, snatching up her purse. "Mom, it's only ten. And yeah, I was, but plans change. There's a bonfire happening, and I'm not missing it."

"Be careful, all right? If there's drinking involved, promise you'll call me. I don't want you getting into any—"

"Mom," Charlotte cut in. She gave Kara a quick hug and

peck on the cheek. "We're not drinking, and even if we were, Uber exists, you know. I'll be fine. Don't wait up, okay? I might not be back till after midnight."

"Okay, okay. But if you need anything—anything at all—call, all right?"

Charlotte was already halfway out the door. "Mom, I'm twenty-one, remember? I've got this." She glanced at her phone. "My ride's here. I really gotta go." She paused, tossing a smile over her shoulder. "Love you!"

"Love you too. Have fun!"

Not too much fun.

Kara stood by the kitchen window, watching as Charlotte darted across the yard and slid into a friend's car. The taillights disappeared into the night, leaving her staring at the empty street, lost in thought. For a moment, she imagined Ethan's truck pulling up instead, stirring memories that left her heart heavier than expected. The kettle's sharp whistle snapped her back to reality.

After pouring her tea, she curled up on the couch, tucking her feet beneath her, the warmth of the mug seeping into her hands. With a quiet sigh, she pulled out her phone and started typing a message to Emma.

> **Kara:** *Em, you up? Had the BEST time with Ethan tonight. But now I'm thinking ... maybe it's time to tell him about Charlotte?*

She took a sip of tea, watching the dots dance as Emma

typed.

> **Emma:** *OMG, details please! So happy for you. Also, if you feel ready to tell him, I say go for it. But no pressure, okay? I'm in your corner no matter what.*

> **Kara:** *What would I do without you? Seriously. Love you.*

> **Emma:** *Love you MORE! Now get some sleep, missy.*

A smile played on Kara's lips as she set her phone down. Emma had always been her constant—a friend who stood by her side through it all. From last-minute adoption events that seemed impossible to pull off to impromptu wine nights and endless *Gilmore Girls* binges when life felt overwhelming, Emma was there. Everyone needed an Emma in their life, and Kara knew how lucky she was to have hers.

Draining the last of her now-lukewarm tea, Kara ambled to the kitchen and placed her mug in the sink. As she turned toward her bedroom, ready to call it a night, her phone blared to life.

She glanced at the screen and frowned.

What now?

She swiped to silence the call, then slipped the phone into her pocket and continued to her bedroom. She'd call her dad back in the morning.

PING.

Why is he texting so late? Can't this wait until tomorrow?
Letting out a groan, she opened the message and read.

> **Dad:** *Kara, Ada mentioned seeing you and Ethan at the diner. Are you sure you want to go down this path again? I remember how he left—no call, no explanation. Do you? And now he's back like nothing happened? He wasn't around when you needed him most. I know you might think he's different, but people don't change. I'm worried about you going through that again. And have you thought about Charlotte? This could turn her world upside down, and she doesn't need that right now. Just be careful.*

Kara placed her phone face down on the nightstand and collapsed onto her bed.

Why does he always have to make everything so difficult?

20

Ethan

Tuesday

Gunfire erupted around Ethan as he crawled through thick smoke, desperate to find his men and get to safety. Explosions rocked nearby buildings. His vision blurred as flames engulfed everything ...

"Get down!" he shouted, jolting awake.

Cold sweat drenched his face as he gasped for air. He sat up, feet hitting the floor, and buried his face in his hands.

The vivid images of smoke and fire clung to his mind.

Hero nudged closer before settling on his lap.

Ethan's trembling fingers found comfort in Hero's fur, his racing thoughts slowly calming. Sitting up, he swung his legs over the bed and rested his head in his hands.

"Thanks for saving me again," he murmured, planting a kiss on the dog's head. "Such a good boy."

As the remnants of his nightmare faded, Ethan reached for his phone on the nightstand. He swiped through his emails, searching for a response from his psychiatrist about his prescription. Nothing. The sinking feeling from last night returned as he remembered his grim discovery: only one pill left. That would be gone tonight.

Despite the early hour, Ethan opened his messaging app. This was too important to wait. He sent a quick text to his psychiatrist.

> **Ethan:** *Just following up. Never got a notification about my prescription. Can you tell me where it was filled?*

Standing up, Ethan grabbed a shirt and a pair of jeans. He dressed quickly and took deep breaths, steadying himself.

It was just a dream.

With Hero at his heels, he walked into the kitchen and unlocked the back door. Stepping onto the porch, Ethan watched as Hero circled the yard, nose to the ground.

"Good *almost* afternoon, neighbor," Clyde called out.

Ethan turned and spotted Clyde sitting on his porch next door, sipping from a mug.

Walking over to the fence, he waved. "Morning, Clyde. Or should I say afternoon?"

Clyde chuckled, raising his mug. "Just brewed some fresh tea. Care to join?"

"I'd like to," Ethan told him. "I really would. But I've gotta get over to the rescue this morning. We'll definitely catch up before I leave town."

Clyde nodded, smiling. "Looking forward to it."

After saying goodbye, Ethan went back inside and made sure Hero's food and water bowls were full, then headed to the bathroom to get ready.

As Ethan dressed following a shower, his thoughts wandered to Kara, the fun he had last night, and how excited he was to see her again—and the broken promise from twenty years ago. Part of him wanted to explain why he never called, to tell her the truth, but he hesitated.

Opening old wounds now? Seems unwise. Especially when we're starting to reconnect. And with everything going on at the rescue ... No, I can't do it to her. Not now.

Heading back to the kitchen, he found Hero munching on his breakfast.

"Gotta run, buddy." Ethan patted Hero's side. "Hold down the fort for me."

As he grabbed his keys and wallet, Mr. Clark, his attorney, crossed his mind. Pulling out his phone, he typed out a message on the way to his truck.

Ethan: *Found a safe. Might have the deed in it. Called a locksmith to get the safe open, but he couldn't do it without ordering tools—might take up to two weeks. I'll let you know when I hear from him.*

Clouds drifted across the sky, offering a brief shade from the May sun, and a cool breeze provided a welcome relief as he stepped out of his truck onto the warm asphalt just outside of Second Chance Animal Rescue.

As he made his way inside, the front desk was empty, so he headed straight for the kennels. The sound of running water and the scent of cleaning supplies guided him toward the back.

"Good to see you finally made it," Kara called out with a teasing grin, waving a mop in the air as she worked inside a cage.

Ethan rested a shoulder against the doorframe. "What can I help with?"

"Well, I'm almost done with the cages," she replied, sliding the mop across the floor. "Changed the bedding and scrubbing down the last kennel now."

"You've done all that already?"

"Well, I've been able to catch up over the past couple of days with your help," Kara said as she finished mopping. "I've even gotten an early start on the next adoption event, too."

Ethan straightened up. "We could work on some of those ideas I showed you last night, give Benny his 'Picture Day.'"

Kara paused, leaning the mop against the wall. "Sure. After all, Benny's overdue for his close-up. Let me just put this stuff away, and we can get started."

After returning from the storage closet, Kara headed toward a nearby cabinet, pulling out the grooming kit. She set it on the counter and grabbed a brush and clippers, handing them over to Ethan.

"Ready when you are."

Ethan took the clippers, nodding as he moved closer to

Benny. "Let's get you looking sharp, buddy."

Falling into a comfortable rhythm, they worked in tandem, grooming Benny with practiced ease. The soft whir of clippers filled the air as Ethan carefully trimmed the dog's coat.

Kara gently held Benny still, murmuring soothing words.

"He's so calm with you," Ethan noted, checking his work. "You've got the magic touch."

Kara smiled, scratching behind Benny's ears. "Years of practice. Though I think he knows he's in good hands with us."

Ethan grinned as he buzzed the last patch of fur, giving Benny a final once-over with the clippers. "Teamwork makes the dream work, right Benny?" He set the clippers aside and reached for the nail trimmer.

"I'm impressed," Kara said, adjusting her grip as Ethan started on Benny's nails.

Ethan chuckled, carefully clipping each nail. "Trust me, it wasn't pretty at first. Got the scars to prove it."

"Scars?" Kara raised an eyebrow. "From dog grooming?"

"Hey, don't underestimate those puppy teeth," Ethan glanced up.

Kara laughed, settling back on her heels as they worked. A few minutes passed, the steady snip of the trimmer filling the air, before she spoke again. "So, what's next for our old boy?"

Ethan finished the last nail. "Now? Bath time."

They maneuvered Benny into the large sink. As Kara lathered Benny's fur, Ethan noticed a stray bit of soap on her cheek.

"You've got a little—" He gestured, then gently wiped it away with his thumb. Their eyes locked for a moment.

Clearing his throat, Ethan reached for the hose. "Allow me to rinse him off, Madam," he said in an exaggerated butler voice, bowing slightly.

Kara giggled. "Why, thank you, kind sir—" Her mock formality dissolved into laughter as Ethan "accidentally" sprayed her arm. "Hey!"

"Oops," he grinned. "My hand slipped."

"Oh, it's on now," Kara said, scooping up a handful of suds and smearing them across Ethan's cheek.

Their playful water fight escalated into a full-blown soap opera, peals of laughter echoing off the walls as they ducked and weaved, flinging suds and spraying water. At first, Benny stood stoically in the middle, but when Kara reached for more suds, he couldn't resist joining the fun, snapping at the bubbles with comical chomps, his mouth opening and closing as he tried to catch the elusive soap. By the time they finished rinsing Benny, they were both damp and breathless from laughter.

As they dried Benny, their hands brushed more often than necessary, each touch lingering longer than the last. Ethan found himself drawn to the same spots Kara was tending to, subtly seeking out those moments of contact. The warmth of her skin sent a quiet thrill through him each time their fingers met—a silent connection that neither seemed in a hurry to break.

After a brief pause, Ethan reached into the grooming kit for the blow dryer. "Ready for the grand finale?"

Kara nodded, positioning Benny so they could dry him

more easily. As Ethan flicked the dryer on, the hum of the motor filled the space, warm air blowing through Benny's fur. Ethan guided the dryer over the dog's back, the fur fluffing up with each pass. Kara followed closely behind, smoothing Benny's coat with a comb. Their hands grazed again, and this time Ethan's fingers lingered over Kara's, gently squeezing before they parted.

A quiet warmth passed between them and before Ethan could say anything, Kara reached up with her free hand, her fingers playfully threading through his damp hair. "Missed a spot."

Ethan grinned, keeping her hand gently in his. "Hey, Benny's getting the makeover, not me."

"Just keeping you on your toes." Kara didn't move, her lips curving into a playful smile.

Ethan chuckled, his thumb brushing over her knuckles as he met her gaze. "I've got a feeling Benny's getting jealous of all the attention you're giving me."

"Pretty sure Benny's just thrilled that you're the one doing all the hard work."

Ethan shook his head, still holding her hand. "Well, I don't mind sharing the workload—or the company."

Their hands lingered a moment longer, their eyes locked.

Ethan's thumb traced slow circles on her palm, and he noticed a shiver run up her arm.

The space between them seemed to hum with unspoken words, and for a heartbeat, it felt like the world had shrunk to just the two of them.

Then—Benny barked, and they both jumped before bursting into laughter.

Kara turned her attention back to Benny. "Well, look at you, handsome," she cooed, running the comb through his now-fluffy coat.

Ethan stepped back. "He looks amazing. I think we make a pretty good team."

"We do, don't we?" Kara agreed, her smile warm. "So, what's next for our glamorous friend here?"

"Time to take the picture. I've got the perfect spot in mind."

"Where?"

"It's a surprise, but we'll need to drive to get there. You up for a quick adventure?"

"With you two?" Kara grinned, scratching Benny behind the ears. "Always."

21

Kara

KARA OPENED THE PASSENGER side door of Ethan's truck, gently lifting Benny into the seat. She glanced back at the rescue. "Are we gonna be gone long?"

"Not at all," Ethan reassured her with a smile. "We'll be back before you know it."

"Oh, almost forgot." Kara checked her pockets. "Let me just lock up."

Ethan started the truck, waiting while Kara locked the front doors of the rescue, then pulled up to the entrance.

Kara hopped into the truck, patting Benny on the head as she fastened her seatbelt.

"So, if we're not going far, are we going to the park?"

Ethan chuckled, pulling out of the parking lot. "Nice try, but no."

Kara tapped her chin. "The lighthouse?"

"Good guess, but nope."

She let out an exaggerated sigh. "Just tell me already!"

Ethan grinned, eyes on the road. "And ruin the surprise? No way."

As they wound their way along the road, the moss-draped oak trees that had sheltered them began to thin out, revealing a more open landscape: nature's own slideshow unfolding before them.

A salty breeze drifted through the open windows, and the vast expanse of the ocean came into view, stretching endlessly to the horizon. Golden sand dunes rose and fell alongside the road, dotted with clusters of sea oats swaying in the wind, and the sound of crashing waves grew louder as Ethan pulled the truck to a stop.

"I figured this would be a great spot for Benny's glamour shots. What do you think?"

Beyond the windshield, a stunning coastal panorama unfurled with a wide, empty stretch of sand and foamy waves lapping at the shore.

As Kara's feet touched the sand, memories flooded back like the tide. This wasn't just any beach. It was *their* beach, where she and Ethan shared their first date. She smiled, remembering how it had all started. She could still taste the syrupy-sweet snow cones, fingers sticky, lips stained with bright colors. They'd spent hours talking, completely unaware of the passage of time, forgetting life's worries—they'd also forgotten sunscreen.

The next morning, they'd showed up to work lobster-red. The entire shift, Kara and Ethan had exchanged secretive glances, stifling laughter as they commiserated over their shared sunburn.

And now, strangely, the thought of that sunburn brought

a warmth to her chest. She glanced at Ethan, wondering if he'd chosen this spot deliberately, if he too was thinking of that day that she'd hold on to forever.

"It's perfect," she said.

Ethan smiled as he picked up Benny's leash, helping the dog out of the truck. "His coat will really pop against the sand and water. Let's head over there." He gestured toward the shoreline. "What do you think, Benny?" Ethan crouched down to Benny's level. "Ready, boy?"

Benny released an excited bark, spinning in a quick circle.

Ethan looked at Kara, then back at Benny. "How about we let him off the leash for a bit? We might get some better shots that way."

"As long as it's not for too long."

"We'll be quick." Ethan unclipped Benny's leash at the waterline. "Okay, Benny? Can you sit?"

The senior dog lowered his bottom, tilting his head as he looked at Ethan.

"Should've brought some treats," Ethan murmured, pulling out his phone.

Kara dug into her pocket. "You mean these?" She tossed one to Benny, who caught it mid-air. "Perks of the job—I'm basically a walking treat dispenser these days."

Kara eyed his phone and chuckled. "That phone looks as old as your truck. No offense, but maybe we should use mine. It's not the latest model or anything, but at least it's from this decade."

Ethan clutched his phone to his chest. "First my truck, now my phone? Ouch." He held out his hand. "Alright, let's see this supposedly superior device of yours."

Kara grinned, fishing her phone out of her pocket and handing it over. Their fingers brushed as he took it, sending a tiny spark through her.

"Well, well," Ethan said, examining it. "I suppose you were right." He aimed Kara's phone at Benny and started snapping. "Benny! ... Benny! Over here. That's right. Look at me!"

Finding a comfortable spot, Kara settled into the sand, her eyes never leaving Ethan and Benny. She watched as Ethan coaxed the old dog through a series of poses. Then, with a burst of playful energy, Benny darted along the surf, with Ethan jogging beside him, capturing the joyful moment.

Kara stood, brushing the sand from her shorts. "Hey, don't I get to play photographer's assistant or something? What can I do?"

Ethan glanced over his shoulder. "Actually, yeah. Could you grab some more treats? And maybe stand behind me—we might be able to get Benny to look straight at the camera."

Kara followed his suggestion, standing behind him, holding a treat above the phone.

After a few more clicks, Ethan lowered the phone. "I think we've got enough to work with. Wanna see if we captured Benny's good side?"

Kara nodded, huddling close to Ethan as he swiped through Benny's photos. They looked at each one together, laughing at the funny ones and fawning over the adorable pictures of Benny. The familiar warmth of Ethan's body next to hers sent a tingle down her spine.

As they scrolled, memories washed over Kara. She could almost feel the rough texture of old Polaroids between her fingers, remembering how they had once cuddled close, choosing their favorite snapshots together.

A gentle breeze tousled Ethan's hair, stirring a familiar urge in Kara to run her fingers through it, just like before. Her heart raced as the closeness between them sank in. Without a second thought, she linked her hand around Ethan's arm, resting her head on his shoulder. The simple weight of her head against him felt like slipping into a memory—like coming home.

Ethan's thumb froze mid-swipe. Slowly, he turned toward her. His free hand reached up, fingers grazing her cheek before tipping her chin upward. Kara's breath hitched as her eyes met his. Those familiar, striking blue eyes—deeper than the ocean at their back—drew her in, just as they had so many times before.

Kara's pulse quickened, the blood roaring in her ears. Ethan's eyes flickered to her lips, then back to her eyes—a question and an invitation in one look.

"Kara," Ethan whispered, his breath warm against her skin, sending a shiver coursing through her.

Almost of their own accord, her arms wound around his neck, fingers threading through the soft hair at the nape. "Ethan."

For a heartbeat, the world held still—and then his lips met hers.

The kiss was soft at first, tentative, but like a spark to dry tinder, it quickly ignited into something more. Heat surged through Kara, every nerve awakening as Ethan's arms wrapped tightly around her waist, pulling her against him.

Years of unspoken longing poured into that kiss. Kara's knees weakened as Ethan's lips moved against hers with a passion that made her head spin. She tasted the salt of the ocean on his lips and breathed in the spicy, woodsy scent of his cologne, carried by the breeze. Her fingers tightened in his hair as wave after wave of sensation flooded her senses, each more intoxicating than the last.

Gradually, the world around her came back into focus—the crash of waves, the call of seagulls, the warmth of the sun on their skin. Kara slowly opened her eyes, finding Ethan's gaze fixed on her, a mix of wonder and happiness etched across his features.

"Wow," Ethan breathed, his arms still wrapped around her.

Kara felt a blush creep up her cheeks. "Yeah, wow."

A wet nose nudging against her leg interrupted the moment.

BARK! BARK!

She pulled back, breathless, and looked down at the dog, then back to Ethan.

"We should get back," Kara said, trying to get her breathing under control.

"Yeah, you're right." Ethan smiled, handing her the phone, then pulling the leash from his pocket and clipping it to Benny's collar. "Time to hit the road, buddy."

Kara hesitated before returning his smile as they started toward the truck. His smile reminded her of the girl she once was, of a happiness she'd convinced herself she could live without.

Their hands brushed lightly as they walked side by side and once back in the truck, Kara opened the window, letting the wind breeze over her warm cheeks. She pulled out her phone and turned on the screen. As soon as it came on, it went black.

Kara groaned, staring at her blank phone screen. "Ugh, seriously? My phone's dead. Gotta have it working for the rescue, in case—"

"I get it." Ethan chuckled, nodding to the glove compartment. "Pretty sure there's a charger in there."

"Thanks." Kara popped open the glove box and reached into it, her fingers brushing past the charger, but something else caught her eye—a glimpse of faded white, buried beneath a stack of old papers.

Her heart stuttered.

Slowly, she pushed the papers aside, revealing the tattered edges. But the image on the Polaroid was unmistakable: her and Ethan, standing on the beach, twenty years ago.

A soft, involuntary gasp escaped Kara's lips.

He kept it?

At the bottom, in faded ink, it read: *Since the day we kissed, I've carried you with me—every step, every mile.*

Before she could fully process it, Ethan's voice pulled her back. "Find it?"

Kara slipped the photo back into place in a rush. "Yeah, got it," she said, closing the compartment and plugging in her phone.

The rest of the drive back to the rescue passed in comfortable silence. Once there, Kara led a contented Benny back to his kennel, giving him an extra pat and a quiet "good boy" before closing the gate. She lingered for a moment, memories old and new swirling in her mind.

As she walked into the lobby, Ethan fell in step beside her.

"Hey, want me to upload those photos now? It might be good to update the website too and make a social post about—"

"Ethan," she cut him off, her stomach tightening. He was so invested in the rescue, so eager to help. Yet here she was, holding onto a secret that could turn his life upside down. She couldn't keep it from him any longer. Not after all this time. "Can you sit down for a sec?"

Ethan paused before sitting on a small bench by the lobby desk. "Sure."

Her gut twisted again, urging her to act. He had a right to know, no matter what her dad had said.

Kara inhaled deeply, her heart aching as she braced for the words that had weighed on her for years. "There's something I need to tell you ..."

22

Ethan

"Ethan, Charlotte is your daughter."

Ethan's body went rigid.

His chest tightened.

A cold shock coursed through him, as if he'd been doused with icy water.

Of all the things Kara could have said, this hadn't even crossed his mind.

She watched him, as if waiting for something—anything—from him. But the words were stuck in his throat.

"Ethan, did you hear me?"

He wanted to speak, but—

A sharp jolt pulled him from the fog as his phone rang. The shrill sound cut through the silence, grounding him in the present. His eyes flicked down to the screen.

"It's Clyde," Ethan muttered, almost numb.

Without thinking, he hit accept and pressed the phone to his ear. "Hey."

"Ethan, sorry to bother you," Clyde said. "Just wanted to call and let you know your dog's gotten into my yard, and he's digging up the garden."

"Clyde, I'm so sorry! He's never done this before. I'll cover anything Hero damaged."

After he hung up, he pushed himself off of the bench and looked down at Kara. "I have to go. Hero got into the neighbor's garden. I'll come back, so we can talk about this. Okay?"

Kara's voice was small. "But you will come back?"

Ethan nodded. "I will."

He turned, leaving the rescue and heading straight to his truck. His mind was racing as he turned the key and started the drive back to the house.

Charlotte's my daughter?

His fingers clenched around the steering wheel.

How is that even possible?

Wait.

He did a quick mental calculation, as he tried to recall if Kara had ever mentioned Charlotte's exact age.

She had to be around twenty, right?

Their last night together over twenty years ago ... That magical evening on the beach before he left town. The memory rushed back with startling clarity. They hadn't been careful, but—

Definitely possible.

His heart thundered.

A storm of emotion swirled in his chest as the pieces fell into place—the timing lining up perfectly.

How did I not know I had a daughter all this time?

The answer struck him: he hadn't wanted to know.

He'd left for the army, thinking it was easier that way—for both of them. He'd changed his number and made himself unreachable, cutting off everyone—Kara, his dad, the town. And he hadn't looked back, not once.

Memories with Charlotte over the past few days flashed through his mind like a chaotic slideshow—the easy conversations, the shared jokes during his volunteer shifts, but not once did he think to ask about her father.

Why would I?

He'd assumed Kara had met someone else, had Charlotte, and then ended up a single mother. He'd dated other women since Kara. It wasn't unreasonable to think she'd moved on.

Now, everything felt—different. Every smile, every laugh they'd shared; it all took on new meaning. He wasn't just someone in her life—he was the father who hadn't been there. And the worst part? He hadn't even known he was part of the picture because he didn't give himself the chance to know.

The thought consumed him, drowning out everything else ...

By the time he snapped back to reality, he was already pulling into the driveway, barely remembering the drive home. Shaking off the haze, Ethan climbed out of the truck and headed over to Clyde's place.

***

KNOCK. KNOCK.

Ethan waited for Clyde to come to the door, but after a minute, there was no sign of him. He knocked again, then tried the door. It was unlocked. Pushing the door open slowly, Ethan stuck his head inside.

"Clyde?" Ethan called out. "You here?"

"Out back!" Clyde's voice carried from the rear of the house. "Come on through!"

Closing the door behind him, Ethan walked through his neighbor's house, through the kitchen, and out to the back porch.

"Ah, there you are." Clyde sat in a rocking chair, sipping a cup of tea with Hero at his side.

When the dog spotted Ethan, he walked over wagging his tail.

"I'm really sorry about this," Ethan said, looking down at Hero.

Clyde waved it off. "The garden will be fine, don't worry. Sit down, why don't you?" He gestured to the chair next to him.

Ethan sat, letting out a sigh. Hero followed, resting his head on Ethan's knee with a soft whine.

Clyde leaned forward, studying Ethan's face. "Everything all right? You look like you've seen a ghost."

Ethan forced a smile as he reached to scratch behind Hero's ears. "I'm fine, just life."

Clyde nodded, reaching out to pat Hero as well. "Ole boy found a hole under the fence. Once he was out, guess he figured he'd try his paw at gardening. Didn't you, you rascal?"

Hero wagged his tail and licked Clyde's hand, looking up at him with innocent eyes.

Ethan sighed, rubbing the back of his neck. "I feel terrible. I'll patch up that hole right away and replace anything he ruined. Just let me know what needs fixing."

Clyde's gaze went. "You know, this whole thing reminds me of Wrigley."

"Wrigley?"

"Your dad's old dog," Clyde said softly. "Robert found him one night, wandering the streets. Took him in, nursed him back to health. That dog, he was something special. Kept your dad company for years after he got out of prison. Even got your old man to put up that fence. I think having Wrigley around gave your dad a purpose, you know?"

Ethan's throat tightened with each word.

He blinked hard, fighting the sting in his eyes.

Doggy door. Makes sense now.

Clyde nodded, continuing. "He'd come over here and sit out on the porch with me, every once in a while, after Wrigley was gone. I think he was lonely in those last months."

Ethan turned away from Clyde, pretending to survey the damage in the garden.

"Look, Ethan, your dad, he carried a lot of guilt. That night he drove drunk, the accident with Sarah Walker—it was inexcusable. A life was lost, a family destroyed. There's no making that right, ever. The town never truly forgave him. But Ethan—"

"He got what was coming to him." Ethan's jaw clenched. "It should've been him, not Kara's mom."

"Ethan, I can't imagine how tough it was, growing up with him like that. You had every right to leave when you did. I might've done the same." Clyde reached over and put a hand on his shoulder. "But those years in prison, they broke something in him, remade him. The man who came back, he wasn't the same Robert who went in."

Ethan's laugh was bitter, hollow. "Well, congratulations, Clyde. You must be the only person in this town who can find anything good to say about Old Drunk Bennett."

"I witnessed it," Clyde insisted. "To my knowledge, he never asked for forgiveness—he knew he didn't deserve it. But he did change his ways. As far as I know, he never touched another beer after prison. It doesn't erase what he did, but he spent every day trying to be better."

Clyde's voice softened. "They say he died of liver cancer, but I know what it really was. That man died of a broken heart. He couldn't go on knowing that he'd never be able to make it up to you—or the Walkers."

A tear formed in Ethan's eye, but he wiped it away quickly.

"There's something else, Ethan. Before he passed, your dad mentioned a key. Said you'd need it someday."

Ethan turned to him. "A key?"

Clyde shrugged. "He didn't say much. Only that it'd be behind a picture of your favorite place. Somewhere special you two went together. Said you'd understand when the time came."

Ethan stood abruptly. "I-I need to go. Thanks, Clyde. For everything. I'll fix that hole in the fence, promise."

Clyde's eyes twinkled. "Whatever you're looking for, Ethan, I hope you find it."

Ethan hurried out of Clyde's backyard gate, Hero close at

his heels and his mind racing as fast as his feet. He knew where the key would be—exactly where.

Bursting through his own front door, Ethan sprinted down the hall, skidding to a stop in his bedroom. His eyes locked onto the dresser, where the framed photo had been face-down earlier. He'd straightened it during his first walk-through of the house, but barely paid attention to it at the time.

Now, he stared at the image—himself at seven or eight, standing with his dad in front of Wrigley Field, about to watch the Cubs play.

As he lifted the black frame and turned it over, something caught his eye. The backing was slightly loose.

How did I not notice it before?

With trembling fingers, heart pounding, Ethan pried the corner of the frame.

There, tucked between the backing and the photo was a small, nearly invisible, black key.

23

Kara

KARA MADE HER WAY to the picnic table outside the rescue, watching as the sun sank toward the horizon, streaking the sky with shades of orange and purple. As the light faded, so did her sense of certainty. With a deep breath, she pulled out her phone to call Emma.

"Hey girl!" Emma answered. "How you doing?"

"Em, I told him. I told Ethan about Charlotte."

"You did? I'm so proud of you!"

"You are?"

"Are you kidding? I know how hard this was for you—honestly, for anyone."

Kara ran her fingers through her windswept hair. "I mean, I feel relieved, but—what if I've made a huge mistake?"

There was a long pause on the other end before Emma's voice came through. "Kara, it was the right thing to do. You've been carrying this for so long—it's time, and deep down you knew that."

Kara paused for a moment, taking in Emma's words. "You really think so?"

"I *know* so. You've got to trust yourself." Emma hesitated, then asked, "So, how'd he take it?"

"He just—left. Said his neighbor called, had to go. Said he'd be back to talk, but I don't know if he will. He never called me back years ago. What if I scared him? What if this was too much? What if he—"

"Whoa, whoa, slow down. Breathe. Okay? He *specifically* said he'd come back to talk, right?"

"He did, but—"

"Okay then, let's give him a chance to come back. Don't jump to conclusions just yet, all right?"

"I'll try. Thanks, Em. But now I need to tell Charlotte. Sooner rather than later."

"How do you think she'll take it?"

Kara let out a shaky breath. "Honestly? I have no idea. Her whole life, it's been this half-truth. We've always told her he left town years ago and that I didn't know where he went. She never really asked much after that, not even his name. I mean, I saw Ethan in the paper years ago, found out he'd joined the army. But reaching out felt, I don't know, impossible? And telling Charlotte." Kara sighed. "I thought I was protecting her. Now, I'm not so sure."

"Listen," Emma said, "whatever happens with this, I'm here for you. Day or night. If you need to talk, vent, cry—whatever. Just call me, okay? Promise?"

"Promise. Thanks, Em. I might take you up on that. But I gotta get going. Anyway, I'll text you later."

"All right girl. You got this. Love you."

"Love you too."

The last remnants of daylight were fading from the sky as Kara lowered the phone, slipping it back into her pocket. She stood still for a moment, letting the weight of the conversation settle in her chest. With a soft sigh, she rose to her feet and started the short walk back toward the rescue.

Familiar barks and whines greeted her as she stepped back inside. The steady routine of feeding and tending to the animals felt comforting as she made her way to the kennels. But her thoughts remained tangled with what lay ahead. As she poured kibble into the bowls, her mind raced.

How am I gonna tell Charlotte?

Should I just sit her down and say it outright?

She poured another scoop of kibble.

What if she hates me for keeping this from her?

She's my whole world. I can't lose her over this.

Kara bit her lip, trying to slow the whirl of thoughts as she began taking the dogs out in the groups Ethan had helped her set up. As she clipped on the first leash, more thoughts struck her.

What if he tells her before I do? No, he wouldn't, right?

What if he doesn't come back?

While walking one group, she mentally rehearsed how to break the news.

"Charlotte, honey, there's something important I need to tell you about your dad." No, that sounds too ominous.

She sighed, tugging lightly on the leash as a dog strayed off course.

"Charlotte, remember how we've always wondered about

your dad? Well, I have some news." That's a little better, but still not quite right.

The hour passed slowly as Kara moved from kennel to kennel, feeding and walking each dog. By the time she locked up for the night, the sky had darkened, and the solar-powered porch lights had already flickered to life. As she walked back toward her tiny house, fireflies danced at the edges of the trail. The balmy summer air and the symphony of crickets would have normally drawn her to the porch to unwind—but tonight, her anxiety had stolen even the simplest comforts.

Once inside, she sank down at the kitchen table and pulled out her phone.

No messages from Ethan ... or Charlotte ... or Dad ... or anyone.

She stared at the screen for a moment, her mind circling back to Charlotte.

I'll just have to be honest and straightforward. "Charlotte, I've discovered something about your father, and it's time you knew the truth."

That's it! No sugarcoating, no beating around the bush. She deserves the whole truth, and I'm gonna give it to her.

Kara took a deep breath, steeling herself for what she knew she had to do.

With newfound resolve, she picked up her phone again, ready to call her daughter and set things in motion.

After three rings, she answered.

"Hey, Mom!"

"Hey sweetie! How are you?"

"Uh, fine. Just helping Grandpa."

Kara's chest tightened at the mention of her dad.

"Oh. Where are you?"

"Shoot, I forgot to text you, didn't I? I'm at the pharmacy. Grandpa got swamped with a big delivery and asked for a hand."

Of course she's there.

Kara took a slow breath. "Oh, okay. Do you know when you'll be done?"

"Mm, probably another couple hours," Charlotte said, then paused. "Wait, is something wrong? Do you need me to come home?"

Kara hesitated. *Should I wait? Maybe it'd be easier if I just held off until later?* But no, waiting had never made things easier. She'd spent two decades waiting for the "right" time, and it hadn't come. *Dad's gonna be livid if I tell her. But this isn't about him. Not anymore.*

"Actually, sweetie, I think I'll come meet you there. Is that okay?"

There was a beat of silence on the other end. "Meet me here? Mom, what's going on? You're really starting to freak me out."

You've made it this far. Don't turn back now.

"It's nothing bad," Kara quickly added, trying to ease the worry in her daughter's voice. "I just have something important I need to talk to you about, and I'd rather it not wait."

"Important enough that you can't wait two hours? Mom, seriously, what's happening?"

Kara took a deep breath. "It's complicated, honey. I'll explain everything when I get there."

There was another pause, longer this time. When Charlotte finally responded, her voice was quiet. "Yeah, okay, but you're really scaring me."

"I know, sweetie. I'm sorry, but I'll be there soon."

24

Ethan

THE SAFE DOOR CREAKED open, and Ethan's gaze locked on the dim interior. His hands shook as he reached in, the cool metal brushing his fingertips before he pulled out the contents.

Please, let it be here.

Hero shifted beside him, as if sensing the change in the air. His tail thumped on the floor, but he remained quiet, his eyes steady on Ethan, as if he too were waiting.

A bright yellow envelope, crisp and official, stood out among the clutter.

Could this really be it?

Ethan's pulse quickened as he carefully pulled it free. For a split second, he froze, staring at it, as his thumb traced along its edges. His heart pounded, and with a surge of urgency, he ripped the envelope open. His hands were jittery as he unfolded the paper.

The deed.

After all the searching, it was finally in his hands.

"Hero!"

Ethan waved the deed, and Hero barked. Laughing, he leaned down as Hero jumped, licking his face.

He rubbed Hero's head with both hands. "We did it, boy!"

Hero barked again, prancing in a joyful circle, as if celebrating too.

Still grinning, Ethan stood and set the deed carefully on the dresser, as though placing it down made it all real. He exhaled, his body finally relaxing.

But as his eyes drifted back to the open safe, something else drew his attention—a bundle of letters, neatly tied with a faded ribbon. Intrigued, Ethan lifted it, his forehead creasing as he noticed the bold, scarlet *Return to Sender* stamp on each envelope.

A heaviness sank into his chest as he examined them, each one addressed to a different army base. As he unsealed nearly twenty letters, his eyes skimmed the pages, and certain phrases jumped out.

I'm sorry for everything ...

Please come home ...

I'd do anything to hear your voice again ...

Each line was like a dagger to Ethan's heart.

The realization struck him hard, knocking the air from his lungs: These were his dad's attempts at reaching out over the years. He shuffled through the letters until he reached the last one—its edges worn, as if handled many times, but never opened. As he unfolded it, a picture slipped from between the pages, floating to the floor. Ethan bent down and picked it up.

It was a photo of his dad, looking surprisingly clean-shaven and put together, standing beside a dog. *Wrigley*, his dad had scrawled on the back. The dog had a scruffy brown coat, and his dad's hand rested gently on the dog's head, both of them looking into the camera with an air of quiet companionship.

His chest tightened as he stared at the picture, holding it a moment longer before setting it down. Then he unfolded the letter, and the words blurred for a moment before coming into focus.

Dear Ethan,

Saw your picture in the paper. My boy, a war hero. I'm proud of you, even though I bet you hate me. Can't say I blame you for that. Most days, I can't stand myself either.

I know I messed up bad as your father. If I could do it over, I'd do a lot of things different. I've got more regrets than I know what to do with. But there's some things you can't fix. I can't take back what happened to Sarah Walker, or the choices I made that night.

Losing my job that day knocked me down hard. After that, I went straight to the bar then passed out in the truck. The nightmares from Vietnam started up again. I was drunk, scared, and too selfish to think straight. Got behind the wheel, thinking I could end my own pain. Instead, I took Sarah's life.

There ain't no excuse for what I did. I've been carrying that weight ever since, and I'll carry it to the grave.

But there's one thing I gotta tell you. Sarah's daughter, Kara, came to visit me in prison a few times after you left. Every time she'd ask if I'd heard from you, if I knew where you were. And one day, she told me she forgave me for what I did to her family. She even prayed with me, and said she hopes one day I'll forgive myself. Maybe God will too. I hope so.

If this letter finds you, son, Kara wanted me to tell you that she still loves you. She always has. I didn't know you had a girlfriend, but she's a good woman.

I don't deserve your forgiveness, Ethan. I reckon I've lost that chance, but I just wanted to tell you one last thing: I love you, son. I always did, even when I didn't know how to show it.

Maybe I'll see you again someday.

Love,
  Dad

P.S. This is a picture of me and Wrigley. Don't know what kind of dog he was, but I know you would've liked him.

Ethan's vision clouded as the words twisted into one painful truth: He'd never get the chance to answer his dad.

The letter fell from his grip, drifting to the floor, a weight too heavy for him to hold any longer. His knees buckled beneath him—he sank to the ground—he pressed his palms against his eyes, trying to stop the flood—but the tears came faster, unstoppable. Sobs wracked his body—raw, guttural, coming from a place he hadn't let himself feel in years.

He hadn't known how much his father had struggled, or how much he'd longed for forgiveness. And now ... *It's too late and it's all my fault.* The finality of it stole the breath from his lungs, leaving emptiness in its wake.

Save for his thoughts, his father's words echoed in his mind. The apology. The love. The years of silence and missed chances crushed him, and for the first time, he let it all in. Hugging his arms to his chest, he rocked slightly, as if he could somehow hold himself together while everything inside him fell apart.

Hero came over to Ethan's side, nudging his arms open and curling into his lap. Ethan took a shaky breath and stroked the dog's fur, slowing his racing heart until the sobs faded away. He buried his face into Hero's soft coat, feeling the warmth seep into his skin. At times like this, all he had left was the steady rhythm of Hero's heartbeat to remind him to keep breathing—and he was grateful for his best friend.

Ethan pushed himself off the floor, his hands trembling as he leaned on the dresser for support. His body felt heavy, like he was wading through thick mud. Wiping his eyes, he looked down at Hero, who watched him in quiet under-standing. "I'll be right back, boy," Ethan muttered.

Hero didn't stay behind. He rose and followed closely as Ethan stumbled to the kitchen.

Ethan's pill bottle was on the counter, right where he had left it. The last pill rattled inside as he unscrewed the cap. His shaky hands trembled as he pulled it out and moved to the sink to grab a glass of water, but just as he reached for the faucet, the pill slipped from his fingers.

Time seemed to slow as he watched it fall, tumbling into the drain before he could react.

"No! No, no!" Ethan frantically reached for the drain,

tried to fit his hand into the narrow opening ... but it was no use. He rested his forehead on the cool edge of the counter.

The last pill, gone.

His mind raced as he pulled out his phone.

It was late, and he knew it wasn't the best time to call Dr. Hartman, but this was an emergency. He sighed and was about to make the call when a new message flashed across the screen. It had been sent earlier that morning.

How'd I miss that?

He opened it and read:

Dr. Hartman: *Hi Ethan,*

I wanted to apologize for the confusion with your prescription. I was out of town and my assistant accidentally called it in to Walker's Pharmacy instead of one of the other ones you preferred. By the time I realized, it was already processed. I understand how hard this might be for you, and I completely understand if you're uncomfortable going there. If you want, I can resend it to a different pharmacy—just let me know where. I'm here to help. Again, I'm really sorry for the inconvenience. Hope to hear from you soon.

"Walker's, of all places." Ethan groaned, running a hand through his hair.

His heart sank at the thought of going back there—of facing Whitaker. But maybe Whitaker wouldn't be working this late. At his age, he was probably done with night shifts, right?

Ethan stared at the message. He could have the prescription sent somewhere else, but that would take time—and he needed it now.

"Looks like we're going out, boy," Ethan muttered, reaching for Hero's leash and clipping it to his collar.

His mind wrestled with the decision as he grabbed his keys.

Just a quick stop, he told himself. *In and out.* Then he'd be done with it.

25

Kara

THE FAMILIAR BRASS BELL above the door chimed as Kara stepped into the cool air of Walker's Pharmacy. She blinked, her eyes adjusting to the fluorescent lights that buzzed overhead. As her vision cleared, she spotted her father's stooped figure at the far end, methodically stocking shelves with bottles and boxes. Kara's gaze swept the store, searching for Charlotte's face, but her daughter was nowhere to be seen.

Kara began weaving through the aisles toward her father when her eyes caught on a man standing near the front counter, his head down, hands inside his jacket pocket. She noted how his eyes darted around the store, avoiding eye contact as she passed.

The hairs on the back of Kara's neck stood on end, but she tore her attention away, forcing herself to focus on the task at hand.

"Hey, closing time?" the stranger called out gruffly, his

eyes darting between Whitaker and the clock on the wall.

"Half an hour," Whitaker said, glancing at his watch. "Need help finding something?"

Kara observed as the man shook his head silently, then turned away from her father, disappearing down the next aisle.

As he disappeared from view, Kara stopped in front of Whitaker. "Dad."

"Kara." Whitaker's eyes widened as he stood up straight. "What are you doing here?"

"We need to talk. You and Charlotte both." Kara took a deep breath. "She told me she was helping with a delivery. Where is she?"

"She's sorting boxes in the back. Look, we're swamped. Can this—"

Kara cut in. "I told Ethan about Charlotte. That she's his daughter."

Whitaker removed his wire-rimmed glasses and pinched the bridge of his nose. "What were you thinking? Why on earth would you do that?"

"He deserves to know he has a daughter."

"It's pointless!" Whitaker glanced at the customer near-by. He leaned in, whispering. "Have you forgotten what the Bennetts put us through? You remember what happened to your mother, don't you? And you want to associate with this man?"

Kara stood there, her heart pounding.

In that instant, she couldn't breathe, couldn't think past the memories. Her mother, the accident, all of it swirled inside her, but she swallowed it down. No more secrets. No more lies. She glanced toward the back of the store, where she knew Charlotte was sorting boxes.

It's time.

Kara took a step toward the stock room just as Charlotte emerged from the back. "Everything all right?"

"Charlotte, thanks for your help. Let's get you paid, shall we?" Whitaker said, striding briskly toward the register.

"Oh, it's no big deal, Grandpa—"

"I insist. Come over here, dear," Whitaker interrupted, gesturing to the register.

Kara stepped toward her daughter, closing the gap between them. "Charlotte, we need to talk. Now."

Her father glanced up, giving her a look.

Kara dismissed it and put a hand on Charlotte's shoulder. "I need to tell you something that can't wait."

She led Charlotte toward the break room. She could hear his footsteps close behind.

As they entered, his voice rose. "Kara, don't!"

She didn't stop walking.

"Go home. I'll make sure Charlotte gets back safely." A warning, a last chance ...

Kara whirled on her heel after entering the break room. "No. I'm done waiting, and so is Charlotte." She turned to her daughter, taking a deep breath.

"Mom, what's wrong?"

Kara hesitated, her gaze falling to the floor as she gathered her courage, but at last she pulled out a chair and sat down.

Charlotte followed suit, while the patriarch of the family stood for a moment before reluctantly taking a seat as well.

"Charlotte, it's about Ethan."

"From the rescue?"

"Yes, Ethan." Kara took a deep breath. "He's your father."

Kara watched her daughter's lips part, but no sound escaped.

As the seconds ticked by, Charlotte's gaze flicked between her mother and grandfather, appearing to search for something—anything—that might explain the bombshell that had been dropped on her.

Kara could almost see the wheels turning in Charlotte's mind, trying to piece together the truth.

Charlotte blinked rapidly, her breath coming in shallow bursts. Her mouth opened and closed again, but the words seemed stuck. Finally, she managed a stammer. "My-my father?"

"Yes, your father." Kara reached for her daughter's hand, but Charlotte's fingers lay still in her palm, limp and unresponsive.

Whitaker threw up his hands. "Well, that's just great."

Kara shot him a sharp glare. "She has a right to know!"

"Oh sure, let's go ahead and tell her everything—the man responsible for her grandmother's death is Daddy dearest!"

Charlotte's eyes widened. "Wait, what?"

Whitaker gestured toward Charlotte. "See? This is exactly why some things are best left unsaid."

Kara slammed her fist on the table. "It wasn't Ethan's fault! I chose to stay out late that night! *Not* him, *me*! But you—" she jabbed a finger at her father, "you dragged Mom out in the middle of the night to look for me. I was perfectly fine."

Whitaker's face reddened. "How dare you! After everything I've done—"

"Everything you've done? Like what, Dad? Control me? Smother me with your 'protection?'"

Whitaker's hands trembled. "Ethan used you, Kara. You really think he cares? He got what he wanted, and walked out, vanishing for twenty years. Now you're acting like it's all water under the bridge? Well, I got news for you kid, the Bennetts are trash, always have been. I warned you then, and I'm warning you now. Ethan is a good-for-nothing—"

"Enough!" Tears streamed down Kara's face. "Just stop, Dad."

She turned to Charlotte, her voice softening. "I'm so sorry, sweetie. You shouldn't have to hear this."

Charlotte squeezed her mom's hand. "It's okay, Mom." She turned to her grandfather. "Grandpa, I think you're wrong about Ethan. He's done great things at the rescue. Even got me to the hospital after my accident. That doesn't sound like someone who's good for nothing."

Whitaker removed his glasses, shaking his head as he rubbed his temples.

Charlotte turned to her mom. "Does he know? About me being his daughter?"

Kara nodded. "I told him today. Right before I came here."

Charlotte leaned forward. "And? What did he say?"

A silence fell between them.

Kara hesitated, torn between the truth and the desire to protect her daughter.

No. No more secrets. Charlotte deserves the truth, no matter how difficult it might be.

"He— When I told him, he just— He said he had to leave because—"

Whitaker jumped in. "There! You see? He wants nothing to do with either of you. I've only ever tried to protect this family. When will you finally listen to me?"

Charlotte shot to her feet, her chair screeching against the floor. "You always talk about protecting me, Grandpa, but from what? The truth? Maybe you're the one who doesn't want to face it." She shook her head, sighing. "I need a minute," she muttered, pushing past them. "Just need some air." She walked back out to the front, letting the door swing shut behind her.

Kara watched her daughter go.

"Look at her!" Her dad pointed toward the door. "Look what you've done to your daughter!"

"I told her the truth!" Kara snapped. "That's all I've done."

"Where are you going?"

"After her."

Whitaker reached for her arm. "Kara, wait—"

Kara pulled out of her father's grasp, intent on meaning what she said, when a flash of movement caught her eye. The strange man was still there—standing unnaturally still by the front counter, dangerously close to—*Charlotte* ...

He wasn't browsing, wasn't leaving. He was just ... standing.

Their eyes met for the briefest moment, and the chill Kara had felt earlier now exploded into full-blown, paralyzing dread.

"Dad?" she whispered, but Whitaker didn't respond.

Kara turned to him.

Whitaker had stopped in his tracks, his usual brisk confidence having vanished. His face pale, hands trembling at his sides, eyes wide and dead ahead with something she hadn't seen in years—fear. This wasn't the father she knew, who always had control.

Her heart hammered in her chest as the man shifted. One step closer to Charlotte. Then another.

"Charlotte ..." Kara's voice came out as a strangled whisper, her legs rooted to the spot.

She could do nothing more but watch the man's hand emerge from his jacket, and feel the weight of her heart drop as her daughter's pleading eyes met the terror of her own.

26

Ethan

THE STREET LAY STILL as Ethan and Hero stepped from the truck and onto the curb in front of Walker's Pharmacy. A faint buzz came from a nearby streetlamp, its flickering light sputtering like the last gasp of a dying star. As they reached the entrance, Ethan's hand hovered over the door handle, but his feet stalled—right where he had last spoken to Whitaker.

The memory surged through his mind once more ...

Mr. Walker's voice cracked as he grabbed Ethan by the front of his shirt and slammed him against the brick wall. His fist twisted in the fabric, pinning Ethan in place. "It's your fault! You killed her! If you hadn't been out with my daughter all night, none of this would've happened!"

"Killed who?" Ethan stammered, struggling to catch his breath. "What are you talking about?"

"Sarah," he choked out, loosening his grip. "My wife ... she's ... she's gone. Forever."

Ethan's knees buckled. "What? No ... that can't be. What happened?"

"Drunk driver. Last night. While we were out searching for you two ..." He paused. "And now Sarah's gone ... because of your little overnight date."

Ethan's heart plummeted.

Sarah? Gone?

She had been like a second mother, always welcoming him, even when it felt like most of the world hadn't. His voice cracked. "Where's Kara?"

Whitaker's face tightened. "After this? Kara doesn't want to see you. She told me it's over between you two."

Ethan shook his head. "No ... no, she wouldn't say that."

"Oh, but she did." Whitaker's eyes narrowed. "And you don't even know the half of it, do you, boy? That drunk driver who killed my wife? It was your stupid, lowlife father."

Ethan felt the world tilt beneath him.

No, that can't be right. He has his issues, but he wouldn't have ... Would he?

"My dad's at work. He's still working."

"It. Was. Him." Mr. Walker's words cut like ice. "Sarah's gone, and you have the nerve to show up here? Listen close, boy. Stay away from Kara, from all of us. For your own sake. I'll mail your last check. We're done here," he said, locking the door.

"Wait," Ethan pleaded, reaching for Mr. Walker's arm but he yanked it away. "I'm so sorry. I never ... I didn't mean for any of this to happen. I'll do anything to fix it. Just let me talk to Kara. Please, sir."

"Anything? Really?"

"Yes, I swear, I'll do anything. Just tell me. Whatever it is. It's done."

"Well, then, if you want to 'fix' things, respect my daughter's wishes. Respect what's left of our family. If you had a daughter, wouldn't you want the same?" He turned away. "Now get off my property. Don't come back. I've got ... I've got a funeral to plan."

Ethan staggered backward before stumbling to his truck, heart pounding. As he peeled out of the parking lot, his thoughts were a blur—Kara, Sarah, his dad ...

Arriving home, he screeched to a halt at the sight of a police cruiser blocking his driveway. Ethan's stomach twisted into knots as he got out of the truck.

Wait. What in the world?

The officer approached and removed his cap. "You're Ethan Bennett?"

Ethan nodded, his throat tight. "Yeah, that's me. What happened?"

The officer's face was grim. "Listen, son. There's been an accident. Your dad's okay, but the other driver ...

Hero's low whine pierced the fog of memory, pulling Ethan back to the present. Ethan shook his head, trying to dispel the haunting images that clung to the corners of his mind. His chest tightened as he blinked, trying to ground himself. With a deep breath to steady himself, he pushed open the door.

The store was quiet as Ethan stepped inside, scanning the empty aisles. He ventured farther, rounding the corner—and froze. His heart pounded at the sight. Whitaker, Charlotte, and Kara stood by the front counter … with a man holding a gun to Charlotte's head.

Before Ethan could react, the man swung the gun toward him.

"Don't move!" the man shouted, now aiming at Ethan's chest.

Ethan slowly raised his hands, his mind racing as he assessed the situation.

The gunman's focus snapped to Whitaker. "You—behind the counter, now!" He tossed a duffel bag onto it. "Fill it with Valium, Oxys, Vicodin, and Xanax. All of it."

With a sharp jerk of his head, he turned to Kara. "You—empty the register. Get all the cash. Move!"

Kara and Whitaker scrambled to comply, their hands trembling as they fumbled through the motions.

"You don't have to do this," Ethan reasoned. "You can put the gun down and—"

"Shut up!" the robber barked, slamming the gun against the counter with a deafening crack. Everyone flinched. "Hurry!" he shouted at Kara and Whitaker. "Faster!"

Charlotte whimpered as she watched the scene unfold.

"You two—on the ground. Now!" The robber gestured with his gun toward Ethan and Charlotte.

Ethan edged forward, glancing at Kara and Whitaker, their faces pale. He slowly lowered himself to the floor beside Charlotte, releasing Hero's leash.

In an instant, Hero erupted into fierce barking.

"Shut up!" the robber yelled, swinging the gun toward the Hero. "Shut that dog up, or I swear I'll—"

Lying on the floor, Ethan reached out, his hand trembling as he tried to calm Hero. "Easy, boy. Easy," he whispered.

But Hero's barks only grew more frantic, each one sharper than the last.

"Shut up! Shut up, shut up!" The robber's face contorted. "Get that dog to stop, or I will!"

Ethan looked up at the desperate man. "If you just put the gun down, he might stop. You're making him nervous—"

"Do you think I care about your mutt? Maybe I'll handle this little girly too."

Charlotte screamed, burying her face in her hands as the sound of the gun being cocked echoed through the room.

Kara let out a cry as the robber swung the gun toward Charlotte. "No, please!"

In that moment, Hero sprang forward, placing himself between Charlotte and the gunman, his hackles raised. Ethan moved, trying to shield both Charlotte and Hero.

"Don't even think about it!" the robber snapped, aiming the gun directly at Ethan. "Or I swear I'll do it!"

"Don't shoot," Ethan said, forcing his voice to remain steady. He slowly lowered himself back to the ground, his eyes fixed on the robber's face. The wild, unhinged look in the man's eyes was all too familiar—Ethan had seen it before, in desperate men in Afghanistan. This wasn't an empty threat—this man was truly dangerous.

The robber's gaze flicked to Charlotte, and Ethan's heart lurched as the barrel of the gun followed.

"Stay down! I'll shoot all of you. I swear I'll do it!"

Hero growled again.

The robber snapped, whipping the gun toward the dog. "What'd I say? Shut your mutt up or I will."

Ethan's pulse roared in his ears, his eyes glued to the robber's finger twitching dangerously close to the trigger. One wrong move, and his best friend or his daughter could be gone. He took a deep breath, his military training kicking in—*stay calm, assess the situation, wait for the right moment.*

But time was running out.

"You two, behind the counter. Hurry!" the robber shouted.

"We're trying," Kara begged. "Please. Just don't hurt anyone."

The robber's eyes darted to the bag on the counter. He ripped it open and stared inside. "This?" he snarled, slamming the bag down, crumpled bills spilling across the counter. "This is all you've got? You're lying! Where's the rest?"

"That's all we have here." Whitaker's voice trembled as he spoke. "But I can go to the bank. I can get you more—anything you want. Just let us go, and I'll bring it back."

A flicker of madness glinted in the robber's eyes as he shifted the barrel back toward Charlotte. "You got thirty seconds to fill that bag, old man. Or else."

A memory from Ethan's days as an Army Ranger surged through his mind—the crack of gunfire, the smell of dust and sweat, the crushing weight of life-or-death decisions. He'd been in situations like this before. But this was different. This was his family—and one wrong move could mean losing them forever.

He knew what he had to do.

Ethan's muscles coiled, every nerve screaming as the robber's finger twitched on the trigger. His breath caught—time seemed to slow, each second stretching out.

It's now or never.

In one explosive motion, he launched himself forward, his fingers grazing the barrel as—

BAM! BAM!

The gunshots echoed in his ears, the room a blur of panicked screams. Ethan hit the ground hard, his head spinning. His vision swam as he tried to focus, to move, but the world had tilted sideways. He blinked, reaching out blindly, fighting against the growing haze ... Where were they? Kara? Charlotte? Hero?

27

Kara

Two Hours Later

The flashing red and blue lights of police cars illuminated the pharmacy parking lot as officers bustled about, wrapping up their investigation. Kara sat on the cold metal step of an ambulance. The vehicle's diesel engine idled, sending subtle vibrations through her legs. Next to her, Charlotte huddled close, both wrapped in scratchy gray blankets. At their feet lay Hero. His head rested on his paws, but his eyes remained alert, darting between them and the surrounding commotion. Every few moments, his ears would twitch at a sudden sound, and he'd release a low whine, as if he were trying to comfort Kara and Charlotte in the only way he knew how.

Kara's thoughts spun as she tried to process everything that had happened. They had been so close to losing everything—Charlotte, Ethan, Hero, and even her dad.

How could things have gone so wrong, so fast?

The sound of approaching footsteps snapped her back to the present. An officer stood before them, notepad in hand. "Ms. Walker, we're just about finished here. I wanted to thank you both for your cooperation."

Kara nodded. "Of course. Is there anything else you need from us?"

The officer shook his head. "No, that should do it. You folks dodged a bullet tonight—literally and figuratively. If Mr. Bennett hadn't grabbed the gun when he did ..." He trailed off, then continued. "The suspect we apprehended is wanted for a string of robberies down in Florida. Unfortunately, not everyone was as lucky as you were tonight."

Charlotte clenched her mom's hand. "You mean—?"

"I'm afraid so," the officer confirmed. "But thanks to Mr. Bennett's quick thinking, everyone here is safe and we'll be taking the suspect into custody now."

They watched as two officers escorted the handcuffed robber to a waiting police car.

"Are you all right?" Kara asked, tightening her hold around Charlotte.

Charlotte gently pulled away. "A little shaken up, but I'll be okay. You?"

Kara managed a small smile. "I think so."

"Where's Ethan and Grandpa?" Charlotte asked, scanning the crowd.

Kara squeezed her shoulder. "Maybe inside? Wanna check?"

Charlotte nodded, standing up and letting the blanket fall away. "Let's go."

Hero trotted alongside them back into the pharmacy. A

few officers nodded as they passed, their footsteps fading into the background. Near the counter, Ethan crouched low, silently gathering the items that had fallen during the scuffle.

Whitaker stopped him.

Kara held her breath as she watched the unexpected interaction unfold.

"You've done enough this evening." Whitaker placed a hand on Ethan's shoulder, his voice unusually soft. "Don't worry about that."

Kara's jaw went slack—her dad showing Ethan kindness?

The moment barely had time to settle before Charlotte rushed forward, flinging herself into Ethan's arms. He held her close, his grip tightening as his shoulders trembled, tears streaming down his face.

Watching them together, the lump in Kara's throat grew. In this single moment, it felt like all the pieces were falling back into place—father, daughter, and perhaps, if she could find it in herself to believe, a family.

"We have some catching up to do," Ethan said, looking down at Charlotte with a tender smile. His words carried a promise, one Kara had long hoped for but never dared to imagine could be real.

Charlotte smiled through her tears, wiping them away with the back of her hand. "I'd love nothing more."

As Ethan released Charlotte, he turned and stepped toward Kara, his eyes still misted. Without a word, he wrapped his arms around her, pulling her to his chest. The warmth of his embrace comforted her in a way she hadn't felt in years—a reminder of what they had almost lost and what was still within reach.

His voice was soft as he spoke, taking in the surrounding space. "You realize where we are?" He paused, a wistful smile tugging at his lips. "This is the exact spot where we had our first kiss. The one we had when we were closing up all those years ago. Remember?"

Kara lifted her eyes to Ethan, the memory of his lips brushing hers rushing back—the reckless abandon of youth, the certainty they had all the time in the world. Now, standing here again, the years between them seemed both a lifetime apart and a single breath. "I remember," she whispered.

Ethan's hand gently cupped her face, his thumb brushing across her cheek. "I thought I was gonna lose you all over again today. Losing you a second time ... I don't think I'd survive it." His voice wavered. "Kara, twenty-two years apart couldn't erase what we had. Not a single day has gone by where I didn't miss you. And I love you. I've always loved you. And always will." His words slowed, as though speaking each one took a toll. "I meant it when I said forever, Kara. You gotta believe me."

His words hung in the air, filling the space between them like a lifeline.

Kara felt the years of pain and distance beginning to fade away. Her breath caught, and she curled her fingers into the fabric of his shirt as she realized just how much she had missed hearing those words.

But the past clawed at her, refusing to let her fully stay in this moment. The hurt he'd left behind when he disappeared. The nights she lay awake wondering what had gone wrong.

"Ethan, I ... I want to believe you. More than you know. But ..." Kara's voice faltered as she stepped back.

How many times had she dreamed of this moment—of Ethan's return, of him holding her—but every dream came with the same unanswered question, the one that haunted her for two decades. Her chest constricted as she searched his eyes, torn between fear and the need for answers. Kara swallowed hard. "Why? Why didn't you call me the night after the beach?"

28

Ethan

ETHAN'S HAND LIFTED TO the back of his neck as his eyes moved between the prescription counter and Kara. "Well," he began, "after everything that happened, I thought you didn't want to hear from me again. I thought I was respecting your wishes."

"Why would you think that?"

He paused, his gaze drifting to Whitaker, standing rigid by the reading glasses display, his reflection warped in the security mirror overhead. The older man's face was etched with guilt and apprehension. "Because," Ethan finally managed, his throat tightening with every word. "I was told that you—"

"Kara," Whitaker's voice cracked as he stepped toward his daughter, reaching for her hand. "The truth is ... Ethan never called because I made sure he wouldn't. It was me. All me."

The confession lingered in the silence, amplified by the

surrounding emptiness. Charlotte, who'd been absent-mindedly petting Hero beside the greeting cards, straightened up.Ethan blinked, his eyes shifting between Whitaker and Kara.

Kara's face paled, the color draining from her cheeks in an instant, like a switch had flipped. Her voice came out as a shaky whisper. "All these years I thought ... How could you?"

"I made a lot of mistakes." Whitaker dropped his head, shaking it slowly from side to side. "And now—now it's the time to make things right."

Make things right?

Whitaker looked up, his eyes red-rimmed and glistening. "The day of the accident, after your mother passed, Ethan came by ..." he trailed off.

Kara yanked her hand away as if burned, stumbling back into a shelf of vitamins.

Whitaker flinched, then pressed on. "And I told him you never wanted to see him again, to never come back here again, to—"

"You what?" Kara's voice shot up. The force of her words seemed to push Whitaker back a step. "What right did you have?!"

"Kara, I—I'm so sorry," Whitaker stammered, swiping his tears with his sleeves. He turned to Ethan and Charlotte. "I was wrong about you, Ethan. Very wrong. And because of my actions, you two never knew each other." He hesitated. "No words can change what I did, and it's unforgivable. Believe me when I say that. Now I realize what I've done, and wish I could take it all back, but ..." Whitaker's mouth opened, but the rest of the sentence never came.

For a long moment, he stood there, as if searching for something more to say.

But nothing came.

With a heavy sigh, his eyes dropped to the floor, then he turned and quietly walked out.

Ethan couldn't let him leave like that and stepped forward. "Wait, don't go," he called after him.

Whitaker stopped mid-step, turning to face him.

Ethan stood still, his heart pounding in his chest. His mind flashed back to all the years he had lost with his father—the words they never spoke. He wouldn't let history repeat itself. Not this time. "Look," he began, his voice lower, more controlled, "I've lost my family once, and I'm not gonna lose this one too." Ethan's gaze moved from Kara to Charlotte, finally resting on Whitaker with quiet resolve.

With deliberate steps, Ethan crossed the room and stopped in front of Kara. He reached for her hand, gently taking it in his. "It's not gonna be easy, and I know it won't happen overnight," he said, his thumbs drawing soft circles over the back of her hand. "But sometimes the best things take time—the kind of time you never thought you'd get back. And we've been given that chance. You don't have to make the same mistake I did with my dad—not if you don't want to."

Kara's eyes, still brimming with tears, met Ethan's. Then she turned to her father. "I want us to be happy, all of us. But Dad ... It's gonna take time and work—a lot of both after what you've done."

Ethan blinked hard as tears welled up. He gently pulled

Kara into him. With one arm still around her, he extended the other toward Charlotte. "Come here."

Their daughter moved into the circle without hesitation, nestling between her parents, her head resting against Ethan's chest. Hero circled them with his tail wagging and nudged his way right into the middle of the embrace, pressing his furry body against their legs, completing the family in his own way.

"Grandpa!" Charlotte called out, turning her head toward him. "What do you say? Are we gonna work through this?"

Whitaker froze, his feet seemingly glued to the floor. His eyes darted between the door—his escape—and the family gathered before him, as if wondering if he deserved a second chance.

In that moment, Ethan saw a piece of his own father in Whitaker—both men trapped by the shadows of their choices. And Ethan knew then, some burdens were too heavy to carry alone. "Whitaker, I know what it's like to think you've lost your family forever. But we're all here now, and we need you. We're family—all of us. And family ... family doesn't give up on each other. Not ever."

Whitaker's rigid posture softened, almost imperceptibly. He hesitated before taking a tentative step, then another.

Charlotte, her arm still outstretched, grasped his hand and gave it a tug, pulling him into the group hug.

Ethan shifted to make space, his arm extending to bring Whitaker into the circle. Then he swept a stray lock of hair from Kara's face as their eyes met over their daughter's head. "We'll figure this out. Together."

Kara looked into his eyes, a glimmer of hope shining through her tears. "You promise?"

Ethan tightened his hold on his family, drawing them closer as he looked at each of them in turn. "I promise."

Epilogue

One Year Later

Kara beamed as she watched Ethan balance on the stepladder, carefully hanging the large banner while their daughter, Charlotte, stood below, arms outstretched, ready to steady the ladder if needed.

"A little to the left, Dad," Charlotte directed. "No, wait—now it's perfect!"

Ethan gave the banner a final adjustment. "How's that, ladies?"

Kara's heart swelled with joy as she looked from the sign to her family, then to the small crowd already gathering outside. Everything was falling into place beautifully.

"It looks amazing," Kara said. "You two make quite the team."

Ethan descended the ladder, a grin spreading across his face. "Well, that's the last of it. We're all set for the grand opening."

The bold letters stood out against the bright blue backdrop: *WELCOME TO THE PETS FOR VETS CENTER!*

Kara admired how the sunlight caught the edges of each letter; they appeared to glow.

"I think it's absolutely perfect," Charlotte said, hugging her dad before reaching out to pull Kara into the embrace. "This is gonna be the best day ever!"

Kara laughed, squeezing her daughter and Ethan, her eyes drifting over to the entrance where the welcome booth stood, festively adorned in seafoam green and sandy beige.

"Speaking of perfect," Kara said, nodding toward the booth, "looks like Dad and Hero are all set too."

Ethan chuckled. "Let's head over and see how they're doing."

Together, they made their way to the booth, where her dad had already settled in, scratching Hero's ears as the freshly groomed dog sat proudly with his new bandana, patterned with tiny anchors and waves.

"You're a good boy, aren't you?" Whitaker murmured, reaching into his pocket for a treat.

Ethan leaned against the booth. "How many has he had of those?"

Whitaker's eyes twinkled. "Oh, just a couple."

"Dozen," Charlotte interjected. "A couple dozen, he meant."

"Are you really surprised?" Kara said, eyeing the bag of treats peeking out of her father's pocket. She slid her arm around Ethan's waist. "My dad spoils that dog rotten."

Ethan chuckled, shaking his head. "You're right—not surprised."

"Well, if he wasn't such a good boy, then I wouldn't," Whitaker said with a smile as he reached down to rub Hero's head.

The sound of car doors slamming and excited voices drifted through the air, pulling Kara out of the moment. She straightened up, smoothing down her shirt with a quick swipe of her hands. "Looks like our first guests are here," she said, glancing at Ethan and Charlotte. "Ready to dive in, everyone?"

Charlotte's eyes brightened. "Sure am, but wait, before the crowd gets too big—should we take a quick picture?"

Ethan nodded, scanning the yard. "Yeah, good idea. Where's that photographer we hired?"

"Were you looking for me?" a voice called out from behind. A man holding a muffin in one hand and a Polaroid camera in the other strolled onto the porch, a sheepish grin on his face. "Sorry, couldn't resist checking out the spread you've got in there." He took a bite of the muffin. "Lemon blueberry—excellent choice, by the way."

Kara laughed. "Help yourself to whatever you'd like. Ada dropped them off last night; she'll be happy to know you love them. But real quick, do you mind snapping a quick photo of us?"

"Of course." The photographer quickly polished off the muffin and positioned himself in front of the welcome booth, raising the Polaroid camera. "Alright, everyone—squeeze in close ... On three! One, two, three ... say cheese!"

The camera clicked, and a Polaroid picture slowly emerged. Charlotte dashed forward, plucking it from the photographer's hand and waving it in the air with an eager grin. As the image developed, she brought it over to Kara and Ethan.

Kara leaned into Ethan, her arm slipping around his waist. "Did you think it was really a good idea to have the photographer only take Polaroids for the event?"

"Maybe not the most practical choice," he admitted, glancing at the photo, "but this way, everyone gets a little keepsake. Something tangible to remember the day by." He pressed a gentle kiss to the top of Kara's head. "Just like we had."

Before Kara could respond, the sound of approaching footsteps and cheerful greetings caught their attention. She glanced up to see familiar faces arriving—Phil from the diner, Ada, Clyde, and Emma walking in with Riley by her side. The crowd grew as more people from Hadley Cove gathered, filling the space with a buzz of excitement.

"Kara!" a warm, familiar voice shouted.

Kara turned, recognizing Katie, the owner of the local bookstore, with Benny by her side.

"Katie!" Kara beamed at the sight of the senior schnauzer. "And Benny! Look at you, boy." She crouched down, reaching out to pet him. "He looks incredible ... a little younger even. How y'all doing?"

Katie's face lit up as she squeezed Kara's hand. "We're doing so well! Benny's been such a joy. It feels like we were meant for each other. He loves coming to the bookstore with me every day, and the customers absolutely adore him."

Kara grinned, standing up. "I'm so glad to hear it! When

I saw how fast those pictures of him on the beach were shared online, I just knew he'd find his perfect home."

"Thanks to you. And thank you for inviting us today. It's wonderful to see how far the rescue has come."

"Oh, it means the world that you're here," Kara said, gesturing toward the open yard. "Feel free to look around and enjoy the day. By all means, make yourself at home!"

As Katie and Benny walked off to mingle with the other guests, Kara spotted Emma weaving through the crowd, Riley happily trotting alongside her.

"Kara!" Emma waved, making her way over. "This turnout is amazing. You've really outdone yourself!"

Kara chuckled, giving Emma a quick hug. "It's a team effort, believe me. I'm just glad the weather's on our side."

"Well, you deserve every bit of this. Riley's already tried to greet every dog here. I think he's the unofficial canine welcoming committee."

Kara laughed, patting Riley on the head. "Aww, we'll make it official next time."

Emma grinned. "He'd love that. Maybe too much. Anyway, I'll let you get back to playing host, but I just wanted to say I'm so happy for you. This place is something special."

"Thanks, Em," Kara said, watching as Emma and Riley headed toward the treats and toys booth, where bags of goodies and colorful toys were drawing a small crowd of excited dogs and their owners.

After walking around and mingling for a while, listening to all the wonderful things people had to say about the grand opening and all the hard work that had gone into it, Kara made her way up to the front porch. She waved her arms to get everyone's attention.

"Hello—hello!" she called out, her voice carrying over the chatter. "First, I'd like to welcome everyone to the Pets for Vets Center, an extension of Second Chance Animal Rescue, where veterans from all over the country will be matched with rescue animals—both from right here in Hadley Cove and from rescues nationwide. Next, I'm excited to announce that, for the first time in a year, all the animals from Second Chance have been adopted. The kennels are clear!"

The crowd clapped and roared, and Kara couldn't help but smile, soaking in the moment, before continuing, "All of this could not have been done without the help of so many people in this wonderful community," she began, "but especially one person I'd like to recognize: Ethan Bennett, who donated this lovely property at 237 Willow Creek Road to us—his former childhood home. Ethan, where are you? Can you come up here?"

The crowd stirred, heads turning as they searched for Ethan. Kara scanned the sea of faces, her heart fluttering with a mix of excitement and confusion when she couldn't spot him.

"Where is he?" she muttered under her breath, her eyes darting from one corner of the yard to the next. She called out again, "Ethan?"

As she was about to step off the porch and look for him herself, a sudden movement caught her eye.

Hero bounded through the crowd, his tail wagging as he trotted up to Kara. The crowd parted, and Hero stopped at her feet, an envelope tied securely around his collar.

Kara bent down. "What do you have here, boy?" she murmured, untying the envelope and then opening it.

Inside was a small card with two words that made her heart skip a beat:

Follow Me.

Kara looked down at Hero, who gave a single, eager bark before leaping off the porch.

She hesitated for a moment, glancing at the crowd. But before she could react, they were already parting, making way for the determined dog. With a soft chuckle, Kara stepped down and followed him as he pranced confidently through the yard and around the side to the back, like a guide leading her on some grand adventure.

In front of her, Charlotte and her dad exchanged knowing glances as they ushered the crowd to follow. Kara could feel their eyes on her, a mix of amused anticipation buzzing around her, but no one seemed eager to offer any explanations.

"What's going on?" Kara said, casting a quick glance over her shoulder. The crowd had stopped short of the gate, some pretending to avert their gazes, others chuckling as if they were all in on a secret.

Kara smiled, then turned to see Charlotte quietly slipping ahead of the crowd, making her way toward the fence. As Kara followed, her footsteps slowed when she noticed Charlotte at the gate. Charlotte's smile grew with each step her mother took.

Kara's heart fluttered as she reached her daughter. "What's this?"

Without saying a word, Charlotte stepped aside, swinging the gate open wide, inviting her mom to pass through.

As Kara stepped through it, time seemed to slow. Her breath caught in her throat, and for a moment, she forgot how to breathe. Where the familiar backyard should have been, a paradise bloomed before her eyes.

A sea of flowers stretched out in every direction, their petals swaying gently in the breeze. Roses in deep crimson and soft pink, sunny marigolds, and delicate lavender formed a breathtaking tapestry of colors so vivid, it almost hurt to look at.

And there, in the heart of this floral wonderland, stood Ethan. The setting sun cast a golden glow around him, making him look like something out of a dream.

He smiled and motioned for her to join him.

With each step Kara took, her heart beat a little faster. The soft brush of petals against her legs seemed to urge her forward. When she finally reached Ethan, and placed her hand in his outstretched one, a jolt of electricity passed between them, just like it had all those years ago. "Where did all of this come from?"

"You haven't seen it all yet," Ethan said. "Close your eyes."

Kara giggled. "Really?"

"Mm-hmm. Close them," he said, gently placing a hand over her eyes and turning her around. "Alright—now open!"

As Ethan's hand fell away, Kara's eyes fluttered open, and the world seemed to shift before her.

There, on the backdrop of the building, a masterpiece unfolded before her.

Kara gasped.

The once-plain wall now burst with life and color, a canvas stretched across the entire back of the house. Brushstrokes danced across the surface, bringing to life the images of rescued animals, their eyes sparkling with newfound joy and their faces radiating an inner light that seemed to glow from within the mural itself.

And then, at the bottom of the mural, the inscription stole her breath:

"Second chances aren't just for the animals we save; they're for all the hearts we heal along the way." —Sarah Walker

Kara's eyes welled with tears as she read the words her mother had once spoken. It was as if her mom was standing beside her, whispering them once again. This mural wasn't only a beautiful piece of art; it was a bridge between past and present, a tribute to the woman who had taught Kara the true meaning of love and compassion.

"Kara," Ethan's voice broke through her reverie. "Second chances are rare, but when they come, they're the kind of gift you hold on to with everything you have. You gave me a second chance at life, and I want to hold on to you—forever—with everything I have."

He knelt before her, taking her hand as he pulled a beautiful diamond ring from his pocket. His eyes shone as he smiled up at her. "Will you make me the happiest man on the face of the earth and marry me?"

Tears streamed down Kara's face as she gazed at the man she loved more than life itself. She nodded, her voice breaking with joy.

"Yes ... Yes, Ethan. I'll marry you."

With a gentle smile, Ethan slipped the ring onto her finger.

Kara glanced sideways at the crowd, still watching in breathless anticipation.

She grinned, laughed, and shook her head as she worked to hold back tears of joy. "Are you gonna kiss me or not?"

Ethan stood, his smile widening. "Of course I am."

In one swift motion, he pulled her close and dipped her backward, planting a deep, passionate kiss on her lips as the crowd erupted into cheers.

Hero barked, bouncing on his paws as Ethan lifted Kara back to her feet, taking her hand once more, and pressing a soft kiss to it.

As the cheers slowly faded into a warm murmur, Kara's gaze swept across the sea of smiling faces around them, then back to Ethan. This was the person she had loved her whole life—the boy she had lost, the man who had returned to her. Her heart ached with the beauty of it all—the years that had kept them apart, the misunderstandings that could have shattered them forever. But now, standing here, she realized that this moment had been waiting for them all along.

"You know," Ethan said, pulling her a little closer, "your mom was right. Second chances aren't just for the animals. They're for people like us, too."

Kara smiled through her tears. "I think she'd be proud of us."

"She would," Ethan whispered, pressing his forehead gently to hers. "And I am too. I love you, Kara."

In that perfect moment, wrapped in each other's arms,

with the sun setting on their past and rising on their future, she realized with quiet certainty that they both felt the same truth: Home isn't always a place you leave or a place you expect to find. Sometimes, home is a person. And, sometimes, it takes a lifetime to find your way back to them.

"And I love you, Ethan."

I hope you enjoyed the story, but your stay in Hadley Cove doesn't have to end today...

Read Katie's story next!

A beloved bookstore, a second chance at love, and a fight to save it all.

At forty-three, Katie Hayes has poured her heart into her beachside bookstore, with her rescue dog, Benny, by her side. As Katie prepares for the bookstore's most important event, her world is shaken by her ex-husband's plans to demolish the bookstore and replace it with a mega-mall.

When widower Sam Carter and his daughter arrive in Hadley Cove, a chance encounter ignites a chain of events that could change everything.

Can Katie and Sam save the bookstore and their second chance at love, or will they have to say goodbye to both?

Get your signed copy at kerkmurray.com.

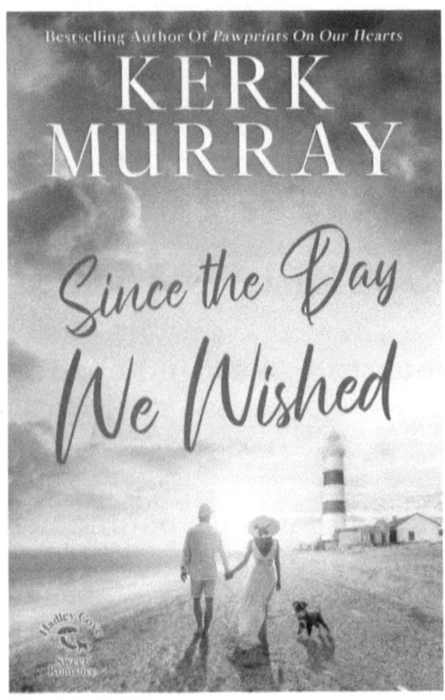

Love this book? Don't forget to leave a review!

Help others discover the *Hadley Cove Sweet Romance* series. Every review matters and it matters a lot. It can be as short as one phrase to a few sentences. Wherever you bought this book, you can use this link to leave an honest review on Amazon, Goodreads, Bookbub, or your favorite retailer:

kerkmurray.com/products/reviewsincethedaywekissed

Get signed paperbacks up to 40% Off

Bundle & Save at kerkmurray.com.

Apply this coupon at checkout for an additional 10% off: **GET10**

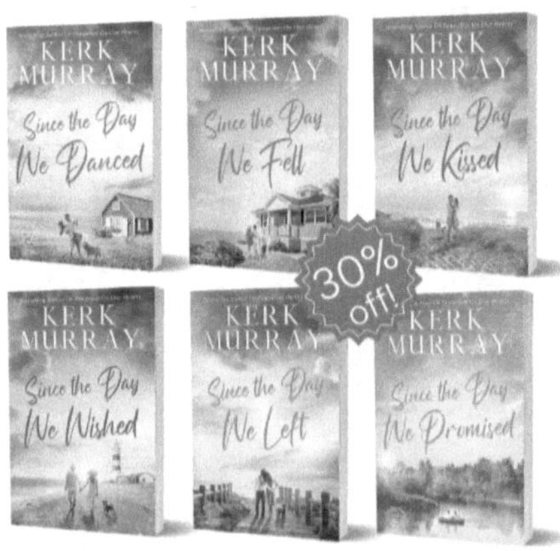

Hadley Cove Recipes

*****All recipes are vegan-friendly*****

Kara's Chocolate Chip Pancakes

To awaken the soul

Ingredients:

Dough:

- 1 1/2 cups all-purpose flour

- 1/4 cup cocoa powder

- 2 tablespoons granulated sugar

- 1 tablespoon baking powder

- 1/2 teaspoon salt

- 1 1/4 cups plant-based milk (almond, soy, or oat)

- 1/4 cup vegetable oil

- 1 teaspoon vanilla extract

- 1/4 cup vegan chocolate chips (optional)

Optional Toppings:
- Maple syrup

- Fresh berries

- Vegan whipped cream

Directions:
1. In a large bowl, whisk together the flour, cocoa powder, sugar, baking powder, and salt.

2. In a separate bowl, mix the plant-based milk, vegetable oil, and vanilla extract.

3. Pour the wet ingredients into the dry ingredients and stir until just combined. Be careful not to overmix; some small lumps are okay.

4. If using, fold in the vegan chocolate chips.

5. Heat a non-stick skillet or griddle over medium heat. Lightly grease with oil if needed.

6. For each pancake, pour about 1/4 cup of batter onto the hot skillet.

7. Cook until bubbles form on the surface and the edges start to look dry (about 2-3 minutes).

8. Flip the pancake and cook for an additional 1-2 minutes on the other side, or until golden brown.

9. Repeat with the remaining batter.

10. Serve warm with your choice of toppings.

<u>Phil's Hashbrowns</u>

To connect with others

Ingredients:
- 2 medium russet potatoes, peeled

- 1/4 cup finely diced onion

- 2 tablespoons cornstarch

- 1/4 teaspoon salt

- 1/4 teaspoon black pepper

- 2-3 tablespoons vegetable oil for frying

Optional Toppings:

- 1/4 teaspoon garlic powder

- 1/4 teaspoon paprika

- 2 tablespoons finely chopped fresh herbs (parsley, chives, or dill)

Directions:

1. Grate the peeled potatoes using a box grater or food processor with a grating attachment.

2. Place the grated potatoes in a clean kitchen towel and squeeze out as much moisture as possible.

3. In a large bowl, combine the squeezed potatoes, diced onion, cornstarch, salt, and pepper. Mix well to evenly distribute the ingredients.

4. If using, add the optional garlic powder, paprika, and fresh herbs, and mix to combine.

5. Heat a large non-stick skillet or griddle over medium heat. Add 1 tablespoon of oil and spread it evenly.

6. For each hash brown, scoop about 1/4 cup of the potato mixture onto the hot skillet. Flatten it gently with a spatula to form a patty about 1/4 inch thick.

7. Cook for 3-4 minutes, or until the bottom is golden

brown and crispy.

8. Carefully flip the hash brown and cook for an additional 3-4 minutes on the other side, or until golden brown and crispy.

9. Remove from the skillet and place on a paper towel-lined plate to absorb excess oil.

10. Repeat the process with the remaining potato mixture, adding more oil to the skillet as needed between batches.

11. Serve hot and crispy.

Ada's Lemon Blueberry Muffins

To reminisce on fond memories

Ingredients:
- 2 cups all-purpose flour

- 2 teaspoons baking powder

- 1/2 teaspoon baking soda

- 1/4 teaspoon salt

- 3/4 cup granulated sugar

- Zest of 2 lemons

- 1 cup plant-based milk (such as almond or oat)

- 1/3 cup vegetable oil

- 1/4 cup lemon juice

- 1 teaspoon vanilla extract

- 1 1/2 cups fresh or frozen blueberries

Crunchy Topping:
- 1/4 cup granulated sugar

- 2 tablespoons all-purpose flour

- 2 tablespoons vegan butter, cold and cubed

- 1 tablespoon lemon zest

Directions:
1. Preheat the oven to 375°F (190°C). Line a 12-cup muffin tin with paper liners or grease with non-stick spray.

2. In a large bowl, whisk together flour, baking powder, baking soda, and salt.

3. In another bowl, rub the lemon zest into the sugar with your fingertips until fragrant.

4. Add the plant-based milk, oil, lemon juice, and

vanilla to the sugar mixture. Whisk until well combined.

5. Pour the wet ingredients into the dry ingredients and stir until just combined. Do not overmix.

6. Gently fold in the blueberries.

7. For the crunchy topping, mix sugar, flour, and lemon zest in a small bowl. Cut in the cold vegan butter using a fork or your fingers until the mixture is crumbly.

8. Divide the batter evenly among the muffin cups, filling each about 3/4 full.

9. Sprinkle the crunchy topping over each muffin.

10. Bake for 20-25 minutes, or until a toothpick inserted into the center of a muffin comes out clean.

11. Allow the muffins to cool in the tin for 5 minutes, then transfer to a wire rack to cool completely.

Riley's Recipe Banana Pumpkin Treats

To bribe your fur babies

*****Please consult with your veterinarian before making any changes to your pet's diet or feeding routine*****

Ingredients:

- 1 cup pumpkin puree

- 1 ripe banana, mashed

- 2 cups whole wheat flour

- 1/2 cup rolled oats

- 1 tablespoon ground flaxseed

- 1 teaspoon cinnamon

- 1/4 cup water (as needed)

Directions:

1. Preheat the oven to 375°F (190°C). Line a 12-cup muffin tin with paper liners or grease with non-stick spray.

2. In a large bowl, whisk together flour, baking powder, baking soda, and salt.

3. In another bowl, rub the lemon zest into the sugar with your fingertips until fragrant.

4. Add the plant-based milk, oil, lemon juice, and vanilla to the sugar mixture. Whisk until well combined.

5. Pour the wet ingredients into the dry ingredients and stir until just combined. Do not overmix.

6. Gently fold in the blueberries.

7. For the crunchy topping, mix sugar, flour, and lemon zest in a small bowl. Cut in the cold vegan butter using a fork or your fingers until the mixture is crumbly.

8. Divide the batter evenly among the muffin cups, filling each about 3/4 full.

9. Sprinkle the crunchy topping over each muffin.

10. Bake for 20-25 minutes, or until a toothpick inserted into the center of a muffin comes out clean.

11. Allow the muffins to cool in the tin for 5 minutes, then transfer to a wire rack to cool completely.

Book Club Questions

If you'd like Kerk to attend your in-person or virtual book club, please contact info@kerkmurray.com.

1. How does the theme of second chances play out for different characters throughout the novel?

2. Discuss the symbolism of the animal rescue center in relation to the characters' personal journeys.

3. How does Ethan's PTSD affect his relationships and decision-making throughout the story?

4. In what ways does the small-town setting of Hadley Cove influence the plot and character interactions?

5. Discuss the role of secrets in the novel. How do they shape the characters' lives and relationships?

6. How does the author use flashbacks to develop the characters and advance the plot?

7. Compare and contrast Kara and Ethan's personal growth throughout the novel.

8. Discuss the significance of Benny, the senior dog, in the story. What does he represent?

9. How does Charlotte's character evolve as she learns about her true parentage?

10. Analyze Whitaker's actions throughout the novel. Do you think his intentions justify his behavior?

11. How does the author portray the complexities of family relationships in the story?

12. Discuss the role of forgiveness in the novel. Which characters struggle with it the most?

13. How does the author use the rescue animals to reflect the emotional states of the human characters?

14. Analyze the significance of Ethan's childhood home and its transformation throughout the story.

15. How does the robbery scene at the pharmacy serve as a turning point in the novel?

16. Discuss the theme of communication (or lack thereof) and its impact on the characters' relationships.

17. How does the author explore the long-term effects

of grief and loss through different characters?

18. Analyze the symbolism of the Polaroid photos throughout the novel.

19. Analyze the significance of Clyde's character in revealing truths about Ethan's father. How does this impact Ethan's understanding of his past?

20. Discuss the role of community support in the characters' lives and the rescue center's success.

21. How does the author use Hero, Ethan's dog, to develop Ethan's character and advance the plot?

22. Analyze the significance of the beach setting in key moments of the story.

23. How does the author explore the theme of identity, particularly through Charlotte's character?

24. Discuss the role of Emma as Kara's best friend. How does she influence the story?

25. How does the author handle the topic of alcoholism and its generational impact?

26. Analyze the significance of the mural in the epilogue. What does it represent for the characters?

27. How does the author use the rescue center's challenges as a metaphor for the characters' personal

struggles?

28. Discuss the evolution of Ethan and Kara's relationship. Do you find their rekindled romance believable?

29. How does the author explore the theme of redemption, particularly through Ethan's father and Whitaker?

30. How does the author use the renovation of Ethan's childhood home into the Pets for Vets center to symbolize personal and community healing?

Giving Back

"Never underestimate the power of a small group of committed people to change the world. In fact, it is the only thing that ever has."

—Margaret Mead

Kerk Murray's readers make a difference. Since the release of his memoir, *Pawprints On Our Hearts*, his generous readers have raised over $20,000 toward the care of abused animals through book proceeds as well as donations to the nonprofit he founded, *The Lexi's Legacy Foundation*. If you feel compelled to donate, you can do so right here:

donorbox.org/everydollarmatters

Here's a list of the animal rescue organizations that readers are supporting monthly through each Kerk Murray book sale:

1. 2nd Street Hooligans Rescue – California

2. Cuddly – California

3. Little Hill Sanctuary – California

4. Love Always Sanctuary – California

5. Sale Ranch Animal Sanctuary – California

6. The Shore Sanctuary – California

7. Viva Global Rescue – California

8. Road To Refuge Animal Sanctuary – Connecticut

9. The Riley Farm Sanctuary – Connecticut

10. Love Life Animal Rescue & Sanctuary – Florida

11. Live Freely Sanctuary – Florida

12. Operation Liberation – Florida

13. SAGE Sanctuary and Gardens for Education – Florida

14. Farm of the Free – Georgia

15. Humane Society Greater Savannah – Georgia

16. Society of Humane Friends of Georgia – Georgia

17. Ruby Slipper Goat Rescue – Kansas

18. Shy 38 Inc. – Kansas

19. Sowa Goat Sanctuary – Massachusetts

20. Angela's Ark – North Carolina

21. Billie's Buddies Animal Rescue – North Carolina

22. Fairytale Farm Animal Sanctuary – North Carolina

23. Blackbird Animal Refuge – New Jersey

24. Broncs and Buns Rescue and Rehab – New Jersey

25. Fawn's Fortress – New Jersey

26. Happily Ever After Farm – New Jersey

27. Goats of Anarchy – New Jersey

28. Maddie & Sven's Rescue Sanctuary – New Jersey

29. Marley Meadows Animal Sanctuary – New Jersey

30. Old Fogey Farm – New Jersey

31. Rancho Relaxo – New Jersey

32. Runaway Farm – New Jersey

33. Troll House Animal Sanctuary – New Jersey

34. Wild Lands Wild Horse Fund – New Jersey

35. Happy Compromise Farm – New York

36. Sleepy Pig Farm Animal Sanctuary – New York

37. Woodstock Farm Sanctuary – New York

38. Enchanted Farm Sanctuary – Oregon

39. Harmony Farm Sanctuary – Oregon

40. Morningside Farm Sanctuary – Oregon

41. Charlie's Army Animal Rescue – Pennsylvania

42. Happy Heart Happy Home Farm & Rescue – Pennsylvania

43. The Philly Kitty Club – Pennsylvania

44. The Misfit Farm – Texas

45. Best Friends Animal Society – Utah

46. Harmony Farm Sanctuary and Wellness Center – Vermont

47. Off The Plate Farm Animal Sanctuary – Vermont

48. Gentle Acres Animal Haven – Virginia

49. Little Buckets Farm Sanctuary – Virginia

About the Author

Kerk Murray is the international bestselling and award-winning author of *Pawprints On Our Hearts* and the *Hadley Cove Sweet Romance* series. He's a romantic at heart, with a passion for celebrating life, love, and the beautiful connections between humans and animals. His soulful stories capture the essence of opening oneself up to the possibilities that love can bring, and the magic that can unfold when we do.

If you're a fan of feel-good, clean and wholesome, swoon-worthy romance stories that will leave you feeling uplifted and inspired, then his novels are a must-read.

Kerk is also the founder of *The Lexi's Legacy Foundation*, a coastal Georgia 501(c)(3) nonprofit organization committed to ending animal suffering. A portion of his books' proceeds are donated to the nonprofit and together with the support of his readers, the lives of hundreds of abused animals have been changed forever.

Join him on his mission in creating a more compassionate world for all living beings, one heartwarming story at a time.

Follow Kerk on social media and sign up for his mailing list at **kerkmurray.com** to stay updated on his latest releases and sneak peeks into his upcoming works.

amazon.com/stores/Kerk-Murray/author/B09C39NLYT

goodreads.com/author/show/21719388.Kerk_Murray

bookbub.com/profile/kerk-murray

instagram.com/kerkmurray

facebook.com/kerkwrites

tiktok.com/@kerkmurray